SUDDEN
DARKNESS

THE END BEGINS

SUDDEN DARKNESS

a novel

MARGOT HOVLEY

Covenant Communications, Inc.

Cover image: *Burning Car* © Luis Sandoval Mandujano & *Woman Touching Brick Wall* © Maciej Laska, courtesty istockphoto.com
Cover design copyright © 2012 by Covenant Communications, Inc.
Author photo courtesy of Erica Michaelis

Published by Covenant Communications, Inc.
American Fork, Utah

Printed in the United States of America
First Printing: October 2012

18 17 16 15 14 13 12   10 9 8 7 6 5 4 3 2 1

ISBN-13: 978-1-60861-144-7

For Art,
come what may

ACKNOWLEDGMENTS

Thank you to past and present members of Writers' Cramp, especially Kendra Fowler, George Hawkins, Marion Jensen, Rosalie Ledezma, Ken Lee, Chris Miller, Christy Monson, Colin Murcray, Caroll Shreeve, Cory Webb, and Janette Wright. You dotted my *i*'s and crossed my *t*'s but, more importantly, showed me true friendship.

It's handy having expert friends when writing a book. Special thanks to Jim Lee, whose career as an army specialist dealing with preparations for an EMP attack made him the perfect person to quiz. And thank you to Shaughn Houtrouw, my favorite FBI agent, for vetting the scene at the Pendleton Pen.

Thanks and hugs to my daughter with the brave curls, Rosalie Ledezma, for the map of Amélie's path. Thanks to my alpha readers—Sande Nascimento, Jackie Smith, and Erica Michaelis—and to my numerous beta readers, especially the teens. Christl Fechter and Tami Fillmore, you were the first to ever tell me you stayed up all night to read my stuff. I had no idea how intoxicating it would be to hear that.

Thanks to Samantha Van Walraven, my hard-working editor who has led me through my first publishing minefield with skill and reassurance.

Thank you to my loving parents, always supportive, always encouraging. Thank you, brothers and sisters, for your patient love.

Thank you, beautiful arrows in my quiver. Happy is the woman who hath her quiver full with such as these. Thanks for being okay with frequent macaroni and cheese meals and for putting up with all kinds of assorted nerdery.

Get Directions

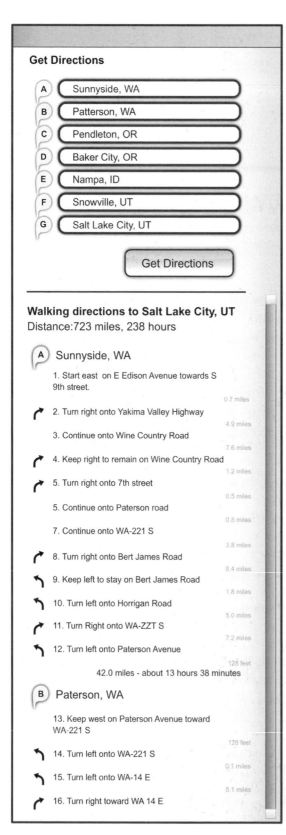

A	Sunnyside, WA
B	Patterson, WA
C	Pendleton, OR
D	Baker City, OR
E	Nampa, ID
F	Snowville, UT
G	Salt Lake City, UT

Get Directions

Walking directions to Salt Lake City, UT
Distance:723 miles, 238 hours

A Sunnyside, WA

1. Start east on E Edison Avenue towards S 9th street.

0.7 miles

2. Turn right onto Yakima Valley Highway

4.9 miles

3. Continue onto Wine Country Road

7.6 miles

4. Keep right to remain on Wine Country Road

1.2 miles

5. Turn right onto 7th street

0.5 miles

5. Continue onto Paterson road

0.8 miles

7. Continue onto WA-221 S

3.8 miles

8. Turn right onto Bert James Road

8.4 miles

9. Keep left to stay on Bert James Road

1.8 miles

10. Turn left onto Horrigan Road

5.0 miles

11. Turn Right onto WA-ZZT S

7.2 miles

12. Turn left onto Paterson Avenue

128 feet

42.0 miles - about 13 hours 38 minutes

B Paterson, WA

13. Keep west on Paterson Avenue toward WA-221 S

128 feet

14. Turn left onto WA-221 S

0.1 miles

15. Turn left onto WA-14 E

5.1 miles

16. Turn right toward WA 14 E

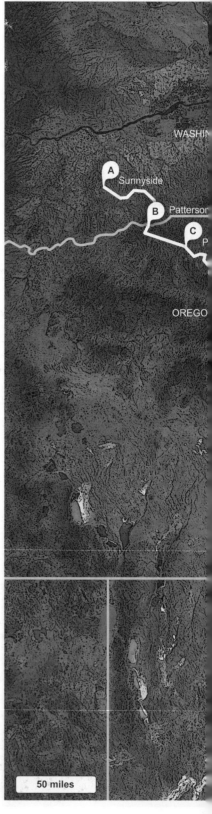

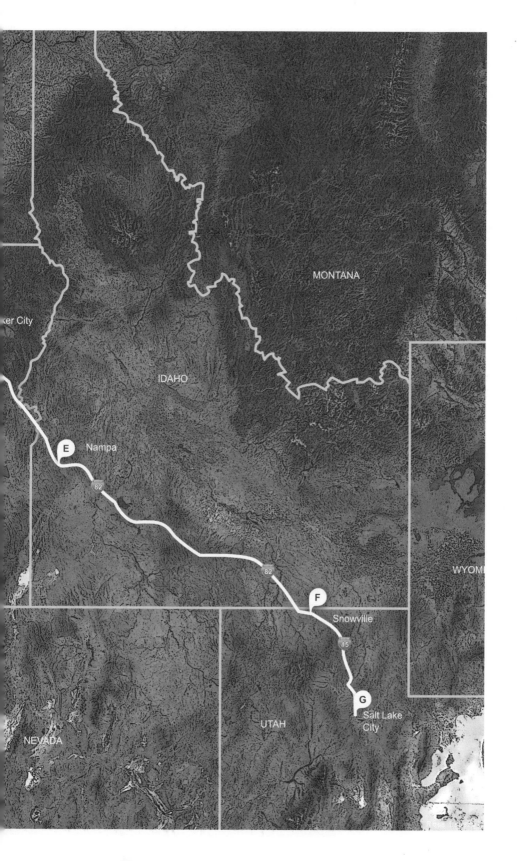

CHAPTER ONE

Friday, May 4

Mrs. Garrett's stare roved across the twelfth-grade Current Events class, searching for a victim. I slouched an inch, just enough to disappear behind George Hill's big head.

"Anyone listen to the news this morning?" the teacher asked.

The only response was the sound of bored breathing and the furtive click of someone text messaging.

Mrs. Garrett looked annoyed. "You're still mine for two more minutes. Stay with me. Anyone? Bombings? London?"

I recalled the radio playing something about that on the way to early-morning seminary, but I'd been too sleepy to pay much attention.

"The bombings were a retaliation for the UK's support of Israel. Seventy-four people were killed, and the power went down across half the city," Mrs. Garrett said.

I thought for a moment about what it would be like to live in a place where things like that happened. Seventy-four people with lives, families who loved them . . . But London was a long, long way from Zillah, Washington, population 2,611.

I laughed inside. Zillah, a military target? Yet a thought flickered in the back of my mind: Hanford. Forty miles away as the crow flies. Hanford's a nuclear power plant, and besides electricity, they make weapons-grade plutonium.

The bell rang. The kids around me came to life, surging out of their chairs. I picked up my cane and hobbled into the hall, which by now was a river of bodies flowing to the gym for a last-period assembly. I attempted to go upstream.

"Hey, Amélie," Zack's familiar voice said behind me.

His family's farm butted up to ours, and we'd been best friends so long he could remember when Dad ran over my leg and crushed my foot. I was little when it happened, so I'd grown up with the idea that I was different from other kids. I couldn't run or play sports, and the cane I used seemed to hang a sign around my neck that said "Weird Kid." I'd turned to other things. I found out I was pretty good at sitting on a tractor seat—or a piano bench. At school, I couldn't bear to be pitied or patronized, so I pulled inside myself. Zack was the only one who got me.

He caught up to me in a couple of strides. "Where do you think you're going?"

"Oh, I thought I'd head home and get started on my practicing."

"Are you kidding? You can play the piano anytime. Hello! That guitar guy is gonna be at the assembly. His whole band."

I reached the front door, but my hand stopped on the handle. Ryan Cook. There wasn't anyone in Yakima County—no, in all of Eastern Washington—who hadn't heard of him. He played crazy-good guitar and had a face that made all the girls sigh.

I sighed now but not because of Ryan and his cute little face. Ryan was all everyone seemed to talk about. "Ryan, Ryan, Ryan," I grumbled. "I'm not into him."

"Aren't you the least bit curious? Why not go check out his skills?"

I stood there, frozen. I didn't want to admit I was curious to see what the buzz was about.

"Lee-Lee." Something soft in Zack's voice made me look up in surprise. He rubbed a hand across his short-cropped hair. "Look, I think it would be good for you to get out a bit . . . more."

I started to protest but felt my defiance drain away under the force of Zack's grin. He took my elbow and guided me back toward the gym.

The room hummed with excitement as the stage crew put the final touches on transforming the place from a gym into a makeshift concert hall, cords winding across the floor in long black snakes. Microphones and loudspeakers arced in a semicircle, and posts with ropes looped between them attempted to keep the crowd back.

Good luck with that, I thought.

Zack nudged me into a folding chair and sat down beside me. Just as we settled in, the room erupted with female screams. There he was—Ryan Cook. I'd seen plenty of pictures of him plastered on lockers and notebooks, and he looked pretty much as advertised. He wore his dark hair longish and curly, teasing the edges of the cowboy hat jammed on his head—one of those straw hats with the brim curling up on the sides. I snorted. I didn't know anybody who really rode horses who wore a hat like that. His white T-shirt hugged his chest, and it looked like he'd spent nearly as much time pumping iron as picking strings. Fake cowboy, fake muscles—I was less than impressed; a guy's got to earn his muscles busting hay.

He thrust his thumbs into his belt loops on either side of a big rodeo belt buckle and grinned at the screaming girls.

Zack bumped me with his elbow, but I rolled my eyes. "Let's hear him play," I said. "We've got roosters at home I can watch strut."

The rest of the band came out, looking like Ryan clones with their funky cowboy clothes and messy boy-band hair. They fooled around with their instruments for a bit, tuning them and fiddling with the monitors and microphones. At last they launched into their signature song, the one the radio stations couldn't stop playing: "Bluegrass Boys."

Lucky thing Cripple Girl got a seat down front so I could see Ryan's fingers as they flew over the strings. I couldn't help staring. How could he move them so fast?

Ryan sang as he played, his voice smooth and nimble. The fiddle player stood with his feet apart, bow flying back and forth in a blur, and the guy on the drums showed them no mercy. The banjo and mandolin players picked away at breakneck speed. Ryan threw his head back and laughed, his face alight with pleasure.

My eyes flew back to Ryan's fingers and stuck there. Despite my determined skepticism, a little ache started inside me. I'd made a halfhearted attempt at learning the guitar but hadn't bothered to spend time practicing. I regretted that for one painful moment before I pushed the thought away. Country music. As if!

Pretty soon everybody started dancing, even Zack. I scooted my chair over to the side so I wouldn't get trampled.

My good foot started tapping, so I forced it to stop. These guys were good and so young. I'd heard Ryan was only twenty. Too bad they didn't play real music.

The song ended. "Thanks, everybody," Ryan said into a stand mic. "It's great to celebrate with you. Y'see, that song just hit the top forty on the country charts, and yours truly and the boys got a big record contract as of today."

More cheering. Then, to my dismay, Ryan's eyes fell on me, the only person sitting in the whole room. I wished I could crawl under my chair at that moment as everyone's eyes followed Ryan's. A murmur buzzed through the crowd.

"Aren't you a pretty little thing," he said, ducking under the ropes and walking up to me. "Don't you like our songs? Come dance with me, baby."

Someone in the crowd squealed, and I saw Zack inching back toward me.

I looked up at Ryan, his tanned face damp with a light sheen of sweat. I shook my head, lifting my cane.

"What's wrong with your leg?"

I stared, unable to form words. Was he really calling attention to my leg in front of the whole school? Everyone already knew all about it in a little school like ours, but I'd tried hard to become invisible. Didn't he know it's not cool to point out people's disabilities? Shame spread over me. The moment stretched out, and finally a girl, Janie Siddoway or someone, yelled, "Dance with me, Ryan."

Ryan shrugged and turned away, ducking back under the ropes.

"Jerk," I said under my breath and lurched to my feet. Brushing past Zack, I pushed my way through the crowd, ignoring the whispers rising around me. The music started again as I banged out of the gym doors.

When I got home, I went straight to the piano and played my brains out.

* * *

I got a few comments in the hallways the next day about Ryan Cook talking to me, including one from Janie Siddoway, saying she wished with all her heart she could be me.

Liar.

The rest of the week flew by. Stares and whispers followed me through the school. People actually seemed envious of my encounter with Ryan. Envious? Of me? What a sensation.

On Saturday I sat with Dad at the breakfast table while he performed his morning ritual of scanning the newspaper headlines. I loved this time with him—my favorite part of Saturday morning. He'd often discuss the events of the day, talking with me like I was a grown-up.

I tapped a headline. "Is that really bad or something?"

"'NATO on Verge of Collapse,'" Dad read aloud. He shook his head. "NATO? Never thought I'd see the day. Sign of the times, I suppose. Could be really bad. You know the bombings in London last week?"

"Yeah."

"Those were warning strikes—telling the UK to back off its support for Israel and letting the other NATO nations know they'd get more of the same."

"Pretty devastating for just a warning," I said.

"Yeah, so everyone's chickening out. The US is pretty much the only NATO nation still staunch for Israel."

He handed me the newspaper and stood. "I'm heading out to hook up the planter. Will you let Mom know? And send Ethan to the shed when he finishes gassing the tractor."

I smiled and nodded, ruffling the pages of the newspaper. My eye caught a help wanted ad. Not that I was looking for a job. All us Hatch kids worked on our farm in the summertime, and believe me, I worked all I wanted to, driving the baler or standing on the back of the potato digger.

> WANTED: Typist. Temporary data entry position.
> One month, part time, set own hours, work at home.
> Computer with MS Word required.
> $15/hour. Call 509-444-0412 for interview.

I happened to be a fast typist—maybe something to do with playing the piano—so the ad set me thinking. I figured if they were all right with an eighteen-year-old, the job was mine to take or leave.

I walked out to the shed with Ethan to talk to Dad about it.

"Well, I suppose it'd be okay, since it's a work-at-home thing," Dad said as he dumped seed into the planter.

"Fifteen an hour beats baling," I said. I started to get excited about the thought of a real job.

I called and set up an interview for Monday. The man on the phone gave me directions to an office in Yakima, the closest town of any size.

I had no experience with interviews—I'd only worked for Dad. I fretted the whole way to Yakima, my fingers drumming on the steering wheel of our old truck, affectionately known as the Bluebird. The truck's stereo only worked half the time, so I listened to Chopin on my iPod.

The address turned out to be in a strip mall, a nondescript office without any business name on the door. The room was empty except for a couple of desks, one with a computer. Several boxes leaned against one wall.

A guy came in, flinging a handful of papers across a desk. He looked to be in his midtwenties, a bit soft and heavy around the middle, and wore Elvis sideburns.

"I'm Amélie Hatch," I said, trying to sound grown-up and professional.

"Uh, yeah." He looked me over, his eyes flicking past my cane. "Fill this out, and then I'll have you take a short typing test."

At least I can depend on my fingers, I thought. I aced the test, and he offered me the job on the spot.

"Okay, this is the deal. See those boxes over there?" He waved a hand toward the stacks. "They're full of mail. Your job will be to open each one and enter the name and address into your computer. When you're done, you can e-mail us the file. There's a couple thousand pieces of mail, and I'd like the job done in a month. More will be coming in as you go, but we're hoping you can get us caught up. Sound okay?"

I walked over to the stack of boxes, opened one on top, and pulled out an envelope. Before I could look at it, the door banged open.

In walked Ryan Cook.

CHAPTER TWO

Monday, May 14

WE STARED AT EACH OTHER, and then, weirdly, we both said, "You!" at the same time.

Understanding flooded through me as I looked down at the letter in my hand, addressed with purple ink and covered with heart stickers. These boxes were stuffed with fan mail.

"You two know each other?" the Elvis guy asked. Ryan didn't say anything, and I finally shook my head.

"All this . . . thousands . . . fan mail?" I stammered. "Wow!" I was making an idiot of myself.

"Uh, yeah," Ryan said, stuffing his hands into the pockets of his tight jeans. "Several months' worth, actually. I'm hopeless about answering it, and now Dave—he's my manager—is going to start a fan club." Ryan had the grace to look embarrassed.

I drew in a deep breath. Okay, Janie might actually want to be me now, just for a month. I was going to be paid $15 an hour for going through Ryan Cook's fan mail?

The door opened again, and a drop-dead gorgeous girl came in, all long legs and blonde hair. One look, and I knew what her job was in the Ryan Cook Company.

"Hey, baby," Ryan said, kissing her briefly.

"Who's that?" she pouted, staring at me.

"Um, she's going to help Dave with the fan-club thing."

"Oh." Her eyes traveled over me dismissively. She, Ryan, and the Dave guy started talking about some upcoming event. I stood there fingering my cane, forgotten.

Finally I cleared my throat. "Is that all, then? Can I get started right away?"

Dave looked at me blankly. "Oh, yeah, sure. Is your car big enough for all this?"

I laughed. "It's a pickup."

The guys had a stroke of genius and carried the boxes out for me. Ryan put those beautiful fake muscles to use, and before I knew it, I was on my way back to Zillah with a load of scented pink letters, no doubt all saying much the same thing: "Ryan U R a hottie" and the *i* dotted with a heart.

When I got home, I took one box in with me and settled down at the computer. I told my little brother Jarron I'd pay him a dollar to bring in the rest. I supposed I could afford that. In moments, I set up a little database and opened the first letter.

Dear Ryan,

I just saw you at the Gorge Amphitheater. You are so cool and I love your music.

Here's my picture, and if you come to Quincy and want to hang out, my cell number is 555-8312. If you texted me I would keep it 4ever.

Write back soon, k?

I entered the girl's name and address into the database. Sometime soon she would receive an invitation to join the Ryan Cook Fan Club. She'd like that, although she'd like a letter from Ryan even better. I looked at the pile of boxes Jarron had stacked against the dining room wall. Not much chance of that.

I did a handful more, carefully reinserting the letters into their envelopes and putting them aside so I could keep everything straight.

Then I read one that made my heart sink. The writer had cystic fibrosis and hoped to have a signed picture to put on the little bulletin board in her hospital room. I had to tell Ryan about this! Even Ryan Cook, with thousands of adoring fans and money starting to bulge his wallet, would want to know, would want to act.

I picked up the phone and called the number I'd been given for Dave/Elvis. His voice mail picked up.

"Dave, this is Amélie Hatch. I'm working on these letters, and there's one from a sick girl in the hospital that I think Ryan should know about. Call me as soon as you can." I hung up.

I didn't feel much like working anymore, so I saved the file and put everything away. My insides fluttered with that anxious feeling I got sometimes, so I grabbed my iPod and went out to the pickup.

My brothers, twelve-year-old Ethan and fourteen-year-old Jarron, hated that our dad let me go off whenever I wanted, but Dad understood how cooped up I felt. Maybe he felt guilty, although he shouldn't. He's not the one who stuck my leg under the wheel of the Bluebird. For the millionth time, I wished I hadn't run alongside the truck as he drove up our driveway from the fields. Why could I have not waited one more minute to greet him? Why did I have to be so clumsy and trip and fall at that exact moment? I'd relived the accident over and over, asking myself these questions but never getting an answer that made sense. All I knew was that what had happened in those five seconds would affect the rest of my life.

I slid onto the seat, popped my earbuds in, and scooted down the gravel road to some moody Chopin, as played by Rubenstein. At the turnoff, I hesitated. Toward town or away? I finally turned the wheel to the right, heading farther out past our neighbors' farms and orchards. I pressed my foot down hard, and the Bluebird shot forward.

I pulled off at an irrigation reservoir we called the Pond, parking the truck by the edge, the fender pushing into a patch of cattails. I settled down for a nice, big sulking session and picked up my iPod. When I pressed its button, it sat lifeless in my hand, the battery drained.

"Great timing," I growled, and flung the miserable thing onto the seat. I slumped behind the wheel. I had no desire to sit there alone, with no company but my own melancholy and no music to cover it up.

I flipped on the radio, hoping it would work. It was set to a country station, and I wasn't surprised when Ryan Cook's voice floated out of the speakers.

Tell it to me straight—I can take it.
Don't pretend, and please don't fake it.

The song was slower than his frenetic big hit and surprisingly sweet. I opened the door and looked around, checking again to make sure no one was in sight. No cars, no people, no one.

I turned up the volume and slid out of the truck. I planted my cane firmly and moved a few steps away from the thicket of cattails.

This wasn't the first time I'd attempted to dance. I'd come out here to the Pond several times for that reason, when I was sure I'd be alone. But I believe it was the first time I'd danced to country music—and definitely the first time to Ryan Cook.

If you mean it, show it,
My heart's aflame, don't blow it . . .

When I was alone, I could pretend I could move freely. My body was an extension of the music, graceful, fluid. I could pretend my movements were elegant and agile. I wasn't lurching around like a Frankenstein. I could even pretend to be in the arms of a handsome dance partner who sang the words softly in my ear . . .

Then I promptly fell down in a patch of Pond mud.

* * *

Zack was hooking up a sprinkler pipe on the little field of hay in front of their house when I drove by an hour later. He waved me to a stop, so I rolled down the window as he jogged over to the pickup.

"What's cookin', Lee-Lee?" He brushed his forearm across his forehead. "Just come from the Pond?"

My heart fluttered. Had Zack somehow seen me flopping around and then finishing off my so-called dance with an exquisite face-plant? "How'd you know?"

"Just a guess." Zack smiled and pulled a cattail out of the front grill of the Bluebird.

I smiled, hoping my face didn't show the relief I felt. "Hey, you're not going to believe this," I said. I had to tell him about the job—we didn't keep secrets from each other. Well, not many anyway. I told him about the interview and seeing Ryan Cook and all and how my dining room was currently filled with the guy's fan mail. Zack's eyes got rounder and rounder as I went on.

"Holy cow, Lee. Are you serious?"

"Yup. Mr. Fancy Pants himself toted those boxes out to my truck." I whacked the Bluebird with my arm that was hanging out of the open window.

"Are you going to tell Janie and Mary Pat or any of the rest of that group? I mean, once this gets out, you're going to be instantly on the A list."

I snorted. "No, I'm not going to tell them. And neither are you, Zackary Allman. They're nothing but a bunch of pretenders. I couldn't care less about that junk."

"Yeah, me neither." Zack sighed.

"Well, come over later when you're done with chores, and I'll show you the letters and stuff," I said. He nodded and turned back to the pipe.

A red Mustang convertible pulled into our driveway right before me. I couldn't think of a single car like that in Zillah, and I knew who it was before I even saw those boy-band curls. Ryan Cook got out of the car as I parked beside him.

I thought briefly about the mud covering the right leg of my jeans. *Who cares*, I told myself.

"Hi," I said, slamming the truck door shut.

"Hi, Ah-may-lee," Ryan said. "Did I say that right?"

"Yeah, that's right." I silently cursed the day Mom had saddled me with such a stupid name. She'd thought it would lend me a little culture, but I'd always hated it. It was way too fancy for a girl living out in the sticks.

"Look, Dave called me about your phone message, and I was over this way, so I thought I'd stop by to see about it."

I repressed a laugh. He was over this way by chance? Nuh-uh. Our place wasn't on the way to anything. Was he that concerned about the letter? "C'mon in. I'll show you."

Ethan and Jarron had left a tangle of irrigation boots in front of the door, which I hopped over with one practiced foot and a flick of my cane.

"Sorry," I said over my shoulder. Ryan wordlessly followed me into the house. No doubt it looked like a dump to him, but I pushed the thought away. What did it matter what he thought of our house?

I showed him into my private office—the dining room—and handed him the letter.

As he scanned it, I took the chance to look him over. I could appreciate a nice piece of manflesh, and he looked good. I didn't mind longish hair on a boy, and I liked the way it curled around his ears and the collar of his shirt. But I was mostly fascinated by his hands as they held the piece of stationery. He had long, nimble fingers, and in my mind's eye, I could see them skipping over the strings of his guitar.

He looked up from the letter. "Shannon Kelland in Kennewick," he mumbled. "I gotta call this girl, don't I?"

He fished a phone out of his pocket and immediately punched in the number written on the letter. I had to hand it to him that he didn't dally, but the letter was six months old now.

I watched the brashness on his face fade while he explained his purpose to the person on the line and then listened to their response. After the other person's end of the conversation, Ryan said, "I'm sorry. Good-bye, then."

He clicked the phone off and stared at me, his eyes piercing. "Did you know? Did you do all this as a set up?"

"Do what?" I asked, shaken.

"She died. She died two months ago."

My hands flew to my mouth. "Oh no."

Ryan hurled the letter down. It slid and spun across the smooth surface of the table. He strode to the stack of boxes and grabbed a handful of letters out of the top. He ripped open one envelope after another and stood there reading for several minutes, silent, letters falling from his fingers like leaves as he glanced through them.

"Ryan," I said, "you couldn't have known."

"I'll read them all, every one," he said fiercely. "If you find another . . . like that . . . you'll call me? Right away?"

"Sure," I stammered, stunned at his reaction.

He grabbed a pen, scribbled his cell number on the back of one of the envelopes, and gave it to me. "I didn't know there'd be stuff like this," he muttered.

His phone chirped an incoming message tone, and he glanced at the screen. "Look, I gotta go. Sorry about the mess. Call me, 'kay?" He banged out the door, and I heard the Mustang roar out of the driveway.

She died, I thought while I scooped the letters from the floor. She died. I put the letters on the table and gazed out the window across the fields, seeing but unseeing.

"Amélie!" Mom called from her bedroom, breaking my reverie.

I leaned around the door. "Yeah?"

Mom sat on the floor, cross-legged, her broomstick skirt fanned out in a circle, making her look like she was floating on a round of crinkled brown. In front of her, a few stubby candles lay jumbled in a basket, a pile of incense sticks to its side. A book lay open across her lap.

"Guess what?" Mom's ruddy face beamed. "Sister Rogers asked me to sub for the Mia Maid class this Sunday."

"Really? Cool." Mom joined the Church years ago, before I was born, but her Church jobs had always been something like ward librarian—to keep her out of trouble, I guessed.

"I really want to do a good job. I've always wanted to teach Young Women," she said. "The lesson's on personal revelation, so I thought I'd talk about dream analysis. I bet the girls would like that. What do you think?"

"Er," I stammered. "Are you planning to use that stuff?" I pointed at the candles and incense.

"Yeah. It'll be great—really catch their attention, you know?" She tossed back her long frizzy hair.

"Well—I know you can't light that stuff in the church. Open flame isn't allowed. Safety reasons."

"Oh." Mom's face fell. "I always get it wrong." She pushed the book off her lap and folded her arms.

I could tell she was on the verge of getting emotional. I swallowed my annoyance. It bugged me that even though she had a rock-solid testimony—converted as a hippie college student searching for truth—she still thought of herself as somehow second-class. No pioneer ancestors and so on, as if that mattered. Sometimes she tried to overcompensate by really getting into the homemaker stuff, but despite her efforts to be Molly Mormon, she never felt at ease with the other women in the Church. Even though she was a bit offbeat and granola, with her herbal concoctions and natural remedies, she was my mom. I loved her. Maybe she embarrassed me once in a while, but doesn't every mom?

"You'll be fine, Mom," I said, reaching down to hug her. She looked back at me with glistening eyes.

"I wish your dad hadn't gone. He'd steer me right."

"Dad went somewhere?"

Mom bit her lip. "A business trip."

"A business trip? But he's a farmer. He's never done that before. Where? When will he be home?"

Her shoulders went up and down. "Not sure."

"Well, can I call him and find out?" I dug my cell out of my pocket.

"Oh, um, actually, he's out of range right now. He'll be able to call later."

"No way," I said. "Seriously?"

She nodded and stood, her long skirt settling around her ankles. Before I could say anything more, she flitted from the room.

Typical, I thought. Mom could be brought to tears in a moment, and the next, something shiny would catch her eye and she'd be distracted. But what was this about Dad? The only time he left the farm was for quick trips with the family to see relatives in Utah or maybe an overnight hunt now and then with my uncles. Strange.

And really weird that he didn't even say good-bye.

The next day after I got home from school, I decided to get right to work. I changed out of my jeans into a pair of corduroy pants and a nice sweater and pulled my long dark hair into a twist. I felt like playing office girl.

I settled myself at the computer and spent a few minutes fussing over things—getting everything laid out and organized. I counted the boxes. There were twenty-three. If I did one a day, I would finish on schedule and have a little time to spare.

Two hours later, I had dealt with two brothers whining to play *Call of Duty*, a restless cat who wanted to sit on the keyboard, and one box of letters. I smiled. This job was a piece of cake, especially if there were no more letters like the one from Shannon Kelland. In this box, at least, I saw nothing but the typical fan-girl stuff.

Ethan and Jarron grumped because I didn't surrender the computer, even after I put the Ryan Cook stuff away. I had a paper to write for school on the life of Liszt, one of my favorite composers. His piano music was so difficult that even after having studied piano for ten years, I was only now beginning to play his work.

I Googled *Franz Liszt* and read through several synopses of his life. I marveled at tales of unbelievable virtuosity, where after concerts, bewigged women stormed the stage, hoping to touch him or perhaps get a snip of clothing or hair. It sounded like he lived the life of a nineteenth-century rock star, with parties, drunken performances, and love affairs by the dozens.

And then I read how, after he grew older and his blood cooled, he took orders as a monk. They actually made him a monsignor, which, as far as I could tell, was some sort of head monk. I felt disgusted, both at him and at the church. It seemed fake to become a monk after all that unfaithfulness. Where was the sacrifice? He'd already done it all. And the church—they took him because of his celebrity, in spite of an impious life. Fake, fake, fake. I threw my notes down and went to the piano, setting aside the Liszt Hungarian Rhapsody. Time for some mind-clearing Bach.

CHAPTER THREE

Saturday, May 19

IT WAS ONLY DAY SIX when I found it.

> *Dear Ryan,*
> *I was wondering if you visited cancer patients and stuff like that.*
> *I have cancer and was hoping maybe you would come and see me at*
> *my house. I live in Wapato. Call me 509-444-8346.*
> *I love you,*
> *Vicki Rosencranz*

I put the letter down and called Ryan's cell. He picked up on the first ring.

"Hello?" Ryan's smooth tenor voice said in my ear.

"Ryan, it's Amélie Hatch."

There was a slight pause. Did he even remember who I was?

"Oh, hi."

"You got another one of those letters."

Ryan swore softly. "Hang on, let me grab something to write with." I heard a scuffling sound and a crash—did he drop the phone? "Got it. Go ahead. Read it to me."

I read the contents of the letter.

"Okay, what do I do now?" he asked.

"Call her, I guess. Set up a time to go see her."

"Good thing I'm home in Yakima for a while," he said. "Wapato isn't far."

I hung up and decided to practice the piano for a while. I'd just opened the *Well-Tempered Klavier* when the phone rang again.

"Amélie, it's Ryan. I called that girl, and I'm supposed to go see her this afternoon."

"Uh, ok. Good."

"Hey, maybe you could go with me. I don't know how to do this sort of thing."

Go with him? That was sure to be awkward. "Gosh, Ryan, I don't know—"

"Please, Amélie. We'll say you're my secretary. Anyway, you are."

"She asked to see you, not me. She's got enough troubles without me tagging along."

"Look. I'm used to working with backup." I could sense his megawatt grin over the phone. I faltered. "Come on. It won't take long, right?"

I caved.

It was almost worth it just to ride in his Mustang. I wished Janie or Mary Pat could see me as I climbed in a couple of hours later. In spite of having open air in common, I decided riding in a convertible was 100 percent cooler than riding in the back of a pickup truck.

We pulled onto the highway. Ryan drove with one hand slung casually across the steering wheel. "Tell me what I should say to this girl. I mean, what do you say to a person with cancer?"

"I don't know. Just talk nice to her. Maybe you could sing something. Yeah. That'd be nice."

"I wonder if this Vicki girl is going to be, you know, all sickly and bald, with tubes and junk hooked to her." Ryan started to sing little snatches of things, trying out this and that. "Something romantic, d'you think?"

"I suppose. That might be more appropriate than something like your 'Bluegrass Boys' song."

Ryan looked at me sharply. "You don't like my stuff, do you?"

"Sure I-I do," I stammered.

"What's your favorite song? Not one of mine but your favorite song in the whole world?"

"'Chopin Ballade No. 4.'" I'd recently decided that was the most amazingly beautiful song ever.

"Ah. A classy chick. Of all the music in the world, she picks a romantic period tour de force," Ryan said with a smile.

It annoys me when guys call me "chick," but for some reason I couldn't explain, it annoyed me even more that Ryan knew the piece.

"Okay, so what's yours?" I said.

"'Bluegrass Boys,'" Ryan said, laughing. I rolled my eyes.

We drove into Wapato—which was every bit as puny and sleepy as Zillah. Ryan turned down a side street, and I felt apprehension creep over me.

"Ryan, I don't know if this is such a great idea, me coming along. Vicki Rosencranz doesn't want to see me." I looked down the road, and ahead, on the left side of the street, I saw several girls sitting on a patch of front lawn.

Ryan nodded toward the house. "I believe that's the address." That became evident as we drew closer. He was obviously expected. The girls jumped up when they saw the Mustang and started shrieking. They swarmed the car.

"Um, you need a bodyguard, not a girl with a bum leg," I said. Ryan shot me a strange, unreadable look. He made shooing motions with his hands to the girls so he could open the car door and got out, a look of grim determination on his face. I decided to stay put.

A girl in a cheerleader's uniform burst from the house and ran toward Ryan. She launched herself at him, and for a moment, I thought she was doing a cheer. She jumped on him, wrapping her legs around his waist. "You came! You came!" she yelled.

Ryan put his hands on her arms and lifted her off. His cheeks flushed. "Uh, I take it this is Vicki Rosencranz's house?" The cheerleader nodded breathlessly.

"Where is she? Where's Vicki?" Ryan asked.

"What? Where's Vicki? Oh!" The cheerleader laughed. "I'm Vicki."

Ryan put his lovely long fingers on his hips. "Did you send me a letter?"

"Of course, silly. How else would you have found me?" She tugged on his hand. "Come party with us."

Ryan's handsome face darkened. "Hang on," he said through gritted teeth. "I was led to believe I was visiting a very sick girl."

Vicki laughed. "Oh, I'm not sick. We just wanted to get you here. C'mon."

Ryan shook off her hand, got back in the car, turned the key, and stomped on the gas pedal. The Mustang leapt forward but not before we heard Vicki call, "Bye, Ryan. It was so worth it."

Neither of us said anything until we pulled back onto the highway. Ryan's face was stiff with anger.

"That wasn't exactly the bedside scene we imagined, was it?" I finally said.

Ryan barked out a bitter laugh. "I can't believe that just happened. Stupid girl. I can't believe she'd lie like that just to see me."

"You'd be surprised what some girls would do."

We didn't talk much on the way back, and before I knew it, we had pulled up in front of my house. Ryan, his hands gripping the steering wheel, watched me get out of the car in my slow, awkward way.

"Don't bother with that mail job," he said as I shut the car door. "I'm not doing the stupid fan club anymore."

I stood there a moment, stunned. "What will you do with all the fan mail?"

"Throw it in the garbage."

I stared at him. What a spoiled brat, I thought. For some reason, all my hurt and anger about being lame, being odd, being left out, being poor, and a hundred other things rose up in my heart like a hot, prickly dart. Unfortunately for Ryan, he was the only available target.

"Poor baby," I spat. "So your little charity project didn't go the way you planned. So what? Get over it. There weren't any news guys there to cover it anyway, so what would have been the point?"

Ryan glared at me. He got out of his car and walked around it until he stood right next to me, hands on his slim hips. As if he thought he was all big and scary, all 5'10" of him looming over a skinny little crippled girl.

I decided I wasn't done tongue-lashing him. "You think you're all that. Where are you right now, Ryan? Huh? You're in Zillah. Zil-lah. You're a phony. A fake star."

"And what about you?" Ryan said, his voice soft but cold. "You're the one who's pretending." He reached out, took the clip out of my hair, and tossed it at me. The sophisticated chignon melted, and my hair fell around my shoulders. "You're nothing but a little wanna-be music snob hiding behind a cane. You're just pretending to be grown-up and cool in your office clothes and fancy French name, the tragic heroine with a limp and a chip on her shoulder. Go put your overalls on, Zillah Girl."

This would have been the moment to flee, leaving Ryan Cook and his stupid car behind as I ran far, far away. But, obviously, I couldn't run. I stood there mute, tears running down my face. I flung my hateful cane on the ground and didn't look up, even when I heard the Mustang drive off.

Everything he said was true. I was the biggest fake of all. I picked up my cane and spoke to it. "You're the only real thing. You're the thing that never goes away."

My mind flitted to the headlines that had shouted from the newspaper every morning since last Saturday—NATO . . . Israel . . . bombings . . . with all that was going on, would any of this garbage with Ryan even matter in a month or two? Did it matter now?

I went into the house, smiling at my mom so she wouldn't get concerned that Amélie was having another one of her freak-outs. A fake smile, but it did the job. I sat down at the piano and played the Chopin Ballade until dusk engulfed the room, my hands ached, and my eyes felt crossed. And then I played it one more time.

I wept as I played. How could Chopin have felt life so intensely at only twenty-five? Had he lived long enough to learn what was real and what wasn't? Did he know somehow that he wouldn't have too many more years to learn before he died?

When the last note faded, I folded my arms on the music rack and laid my head on them, letting my tears drip into my sweater. Then I heard a tap and a whisper.

"Lee . . . Lee . . ." A familiar voice floated through the window behind the piano. Zack's voice.

I grabbed a jacket and slipped outside. Zack waited under the huge old elms edging the driveway. Even though Zack didn't share my love of Chopin, his presence was in its own way just as comforting. As children, we'd crept out late at night many times, pretending to hunt critters or just to look at the stars, but it'd been a long, long time since then.

Late spring air seeped into my jacket, almost too cold to be comfortable. Moonlight slanted across Zack's face, and I gazed at his familiar features. I knew every inch of his face—the way his nose crinkled across the bridge when he smiled, the cowlick in his hair on the left, the way he put his tongue between his teeth when he was thinking.

We walked across the yard to the irrigation canal that ran along the western edge of the grass and sat down on a ledge of concrete that jutted out over a pump. I looked down at the gently flowing water and wondered why a man-made river, with concrete sides and no banks, made this such a nice spot to sit. Trees arched overhead, and a light my dad had anchored into a tree (aimed at the pump to help with late-night water chores) cast a dreamlike glow over us.

Zack's eyes searched mine. "What's making you sad, Lee-Lee?" he asked. "Just that old blue feeling you get?"

"I'm not sad, Zack. Not anymore."

He smiled that smile I'd grown up with.

Stars studded the sky above us, and I breathed in the cold, crisp air as deeply as I could.

It felt real.

I looked back at Zack in wonderment. Something almost like a zing of electricity passed between us. What was that feeling? Zack and I . . . I'd never thought of us in *that* way. He was my oldest, best friend, a rock-steady fixture in my life. So why did my mind wander toward the thought of his shoulders, broad and strong beneath his sweatshirt?

I smiled back and felt Zack relax. He'd been worrying about me, like he always did. He knew better than anyone how blue moods would take me now and then.

"That's my girl," he said. "Thanks for coming out with me. I know you have to get up early for that church thing . . . seminole or seminism or whatever."

"Cemetery," I corrected him and laughed.

"What do you do there anyway? It's like catechism, right?"

My breath caught. Zack and his dad were casual Catholics. They went to church on Christmas Eve and maybe a couple other times each year. But long ago, his dad had made it very clear: in order for Zack to be friends with me, we could not discuss religion. Period.

I'd waited a long time for a question like this. After all, in Primary, the teachers had taught us to look for nonmember friends we could share the gospel with. And the first person I always thought of was Zack. The *only* person I thought of was Zack. But I'd never crossed the line his dad had drawn.

I sorted through various ways to answer him. He hadn't asked me to expound on doctrine, so I decided on a casual reply.

At that moment, the light in the tree above us winked out.

For a second, I thought of my brothers, who liked nothing better than to tease and torment me. If they'd noticed me sitting out here with Zack, they'd immediately trip the switch, snickering the whole time. But as I looked over my shoulder at the house, it crouched in complete darkness. In fact, there were no lights anywhere.

Zack sprang to his feet. "Look!" he pointed toward the valley to the south, where we could normally see the lights from Zillah glimmering faintly in the distance. But now, there was only dark.

A curious dread crept over me. I stood and moved closer to Zack. "What happened?"

"A blackout, I guess." The country could be very quiet at night, but now it seemed especially dark and silent. I realized the pump had shut off, subtracting a sound I hadn't even noticed before.

"Ah-may-leeeeeeee." Mom's voice floated over from the house. "Where are you? Come quick. The power's gone off."

"No duh," I said, but, of course, only Zack could hear me. I didn't talk sassy to Mom—at least not so she could hear.

"I better go see about things at our place," Zack said. "I'll check on you guys later. Your dad still gone?"

I nodded, and Zack vanished into the shrouded trees lining the driveway. I limped across the yard and into the house.

Mom stood in the entry, wringing her hands like a Victorian heroine. "There you are. What were you doing outside? I was worried about you. Nothing works—your father's not here—"

"Where's that basket of candles?" I said, moving past her.

"Power's out, power's out," Ethan sang from the kitchen. The smell of natural gas invaded my senses.

"Ethan! Stop fooling with the stove!" I yelled. "Smell that gas?"

"Weird. Thought it would light," Ethan said. "It's a gas stove, not electric. Why doesn't it work?"

"It has electric igniters. We could light it with a match if we needed to. But for now, stop filling the house with nasty gas, okay?"

"Where's Jarron?" Mom asked, thrusting the basket of candles into my hands.

"Over here," Jarron called from the family room. "We were playing Mario Kart when everything went off. Didn't even give us a chance to save our game."

I fumbled for the box of matches from the cupboard by the sink and struck one, the little flame blazing to life and illuminating the basket of fat candles. I quickly lit one and handed it to Mom. She clutched it as if having something for her hands to do was all she needed. Shadows danced across her face.

"At least we're all accounted for," I said. "Well, all but Dad. Where is he, Mom? When's he coming home?"

"I don't know. Ask the bishop."

"The bishop! Why in the world would he know?" I lit a few more candles and set them around on the kitchen counters. My brothers drew into the circle of light, attracted to their flicker like a couple of bugs.

"He's the one who set up this trip."

"The bishop?" I said again. That made no sense. The bishop was a farmer like us. Why would he set up a business trip for Dad? "This is a business thing, not a Church thing?"

"I guess," Mom said.

It didn't make sense for it to be a Church thing either. Dad was the Scoutmaster for our ward and had been for years. Sometimes the Scouts went on trips but usually not in the spring, and my brothers, the mainstays of the troop, stood right there looking at me. If there had been a Scout trip, they'd be gone as well.

To be sure, I asked them. "Any Scout stuff going on that you know of?"

Jarron and Ethan both shrugged.

I growled to myself. "Oh well. I guess I'm going to bed. Not much else to do."

"I'm sure the power will come back on by morning. Take a candle, but blow it out before you go to sleep. Let's not burn down the house," Mom said.

I crept to my room, the candle casting huge distorted shadows on the wall. I stumbled over Jarron's shoes as I made my way to the bathroom. I used only a tiny splash of water on my toothbrush. Last year the well pump had gone out, and from that experience, I knew we'd only have running water until the water in the lines was used.

I set the candle on my nightstand and crawled under my blankets. I stared into its golden glow, my thoughts flitting back to Zack. Had he felt the same thing I had? I puffed out the flame. My mind replayed the scene over and over, searching for clues until sleep overtook me.

In the morning, the power was still out. I limped through the quiet house, lit only by the weak light of dawn through the windows.

Mom stood at the kitchen window, and Ethan and Jarron stumbled in, their hair all awry from sleep. "We've got to figure out whether or not they cancelled school," she said. "Last night it looked like the blackout extended over the whole valley, but maybe the power's back on in town."

Obviously we couldn't switch on the TV to check. We fumbled around for batteries for a radio and found only the wrong sizes.

"Hey, isn't there a crank-powered radio in the seventy-two-hour kit?" Ethan said. He ran to fetch it from its place on a shelf in the milk barn.

Mom smiled, pulling the milk jug from the not-so-cool fridge. "Drink up, kids. This milk won't last."

When Ethan got back with the kit, we dug through the contents, the boys clustered around them in fascination, fighting over the privilege of cranking the radio once we found it. While they cranked, I fiddled the dial. I went all the way up and back, but we heard nothing but the crackle of static. None of the Yakima stations seemed to be broadcasting.

So this extends to Yakima, I thought. Odd.

I turned the dial through its range one more time, inching along the band. I finally picked up a faint voice and homed in on it.

". . . the Tri-City area. Repeat: Warning. Do not attempt to travel into the Tri-City area. Possible leak and/or contamination at Hanford. Roads in southeastern Washington should be considered unsafe, especially in the Tri-City area." Then the message looped.

Holy cow! A leak at Hanford? Was radiation invisibly seeping toward us at that very moment? What did it have to do with the power being down?

CHAPTER FOUR

Monday, May 21

JARRON AND ETHAN TROOPED OUT for morning chores, leaving Mom and me to our bowls of Kashi.

After we finished eating, Mom and I took everything out of the little freezer above the fridge and put it in the deep freeze. It still seemed pretty cold, but another day or so and stuff would thaw. Surely by then this power thing would be straightened out. We'd had outages for a few hours before, and here and there a longer spell of a day or so, but nothing more. Still, the radio message gave me butterflies in my gut.

Mom and I went out and sat on our swing on the front porch. I held a hank of yarn between my hands while she wound it into a ball. A fitting activity, I supposed, for a farmhouse without electricity. Next I'd be churning butter or something. Ha.

A little before noon, Zack and his dad came over.

"Mrs. Hatch, how are you faring over here? We thought we'd check on you, with your man gone and all. Anything need doing?" Frank Allman said.

"Thanks, Frank, but we're fine. The power will be on directly, I'm sure, and Loren will be home soon. I appreciate the gesture." Mom smiled brightly, tucking a stray frizzy lock behind one ear.

Zack looked at me, flicking his eyes up and then over. His message was clear: *follow me out.*

"Be right back, Mom," I said, carefully stepping off the porch. I left my cane lying against the porch swing. I'd have Zack to hold onto if I got unsteady.

Frank tossed us a smile and strode back toward his place, leaving us to walk at an Amélie pace under the budding trees edging the drive.

"Okay, I know your mom wants to be her own girl and everything, but tell me for real. How can we help?" Zack said.

"We're fine. For real," I replied. I noticed how nice my hand felt on his arm, although it had sat there a hundred times before. "I did hear something freaky on the radio though."

"Hanford?"

"Yeah."

He nodded. "We heard that too. Crazy."

"I wonder what it means. I mean, are we far enough away? Are we safe?"

"Oh yeah. I'm sure we're fine. You know the government would be on top of that kind of thing. Just no trips to the Tri-Cities, okay?" He winked at me.

I laughed. "Deal."

We turned around, and Zack walked me back to my waiting cane. "Just send a brother a'running if you need anything."

"Okay."

"Promise?"

"Sure."

Zack waved and trotted away. I stood and watched until the curve of the drive hid him from my eyes.

The day stretched into evening and still no power. We lit the candles again and heated some canned soup on the stove after lighting the pilot with a match. The boys acted restless with no Xbox or computer, but they seemed to look on it as an adventure. We found a lantern in the camping gear for them to use for night chores, and afterward they settled down for a card game of War. I went back outside.

I'd been waiting for dark so I could check if power had come back on anywhere within my sight. I scanned the valley, turning slowly in place. No light. No light anywhere. The crank radio still played nothing at all but that weird looping message.

* * *

The next morning was Tuesday. We cranked the radio again, and this time I could hear other garbled voices, too faint to make out. I wondered for the hundredth time how far the blackout reached. Had it touched any big cities like Seattle or Los Angeles? What would it be like to ride out a power outage in a city? So far, we'd only been a little inconvenienced. We had a typical Mormon pantry—enough food to keep us for a good long time, even if we did lose the food in the freezer. We had our own well that Dad had equipped with a hand pump for a time like this. If it weren't for the Hanford thing, I'd probably think of it as a fun break from school.

Zack had to be right. We lived plenty far away from Hanford, with all its barbwire and soldiers . . . fences that kept things from getting in, but I couldn't help but think a little uneasily that they did nothing to keep stuff from getting out.

I checked the deep freezer that held a couple hundred dollars' worth of meat, which was definitely starting to thaw. We owned a generator and even our own supply of gas we could use to run it with. As long as the situation was temporary, it seemed a good idea to fire it up and save the food in the freezer.

The gas tank was out behind the barn, set on a frame that held it five feet off the ground. A gas truck came around and filled it every couple of months, and I suppose it held a few hundred gallons. I had Jarron fill the generator and bring it up to the house. He got it going, and we plugged the freezer in. The sound of the thing was near deafening, especially after the intense quiet of the last couple of days. I fled for my bedroom after forbidding the boys to plug anything else into the generator.

I sat on the edge of my bed and tried to drive all the worry out of my head. What if this went on and on? I pictured us getting to the point where we'd have to burn stuff to keep warm and cook with. Well, there was still a big stack of fan letters in the dining room that would make great kindling. I laughed.

I remembered how outraged I'd been that Ryan had planned to throw all of those letters out. How silly and unimportant that seemed now.

I didn't like the closed-in feeling this power outage gave me. I'd become somewhat adept at avoiding stuff that reminded me I was a useless cripple girl, but it seemed like every time I turned around, something happened that underlined my disability with a bright fluorescent highlighter.

The solid, dependable pillar of my teenage life, my dad, was strangely, oddly, inexplicably gone—as if someone hit the delete key. Poof.

"Maylee!" Mom's voice floated down the hall. "Where're the keys to the Bluebird?"

"Where are you off to?" I asked, meeting her in the hall.

"I'm going to drive over to the bishop's, and he's going to tell me when your dad is coming home. There has to be a way to contact him. This is getting ridiculous."

Not a bad idea. I reached for my jacket to fish out the keys when I heard wheels crunch on the gravel drive.

"Who's that?" I asked, my heart skipping. Was Dad home at last?

Mom smiled as she looked out the window. "Speak of the devil. It's the bishop."

"Are you kidding?" But sure enough, Bishop Taylor trundled up to our door, his lumpy frame swathed in a plaid flannel shirt and dirty jeans, wet around the bottom. He'd obviously come straight from his fields.

Mom flung open the door, and we both stepped onto the porch. "Hello, Bishop. Good timing. I was just on my way over to see you." She motioned to the porch swing.

Bishop Taylor shook her hand, nodded at me, and sat down. I stayed where I was, hanging onto the doorframe.

"Hi, ladies. How are you holding up?"

"We're fine. But we're very anxious about Loren. We haven't heard a peep from him. Have you?"

Bishop Taylor shook his grizzled head. "I haven't. I'm sorry I don't know more. I'm stopping around at all the homes in the ward, to check on everyone and to give you an important message from the stake president."

"Oh. A message." Disappointment creased Mom's face.

"The stake president asked me to pass along his concern. And he's called a meeting. It's very important that you be there. Tonight, five o'clock, at the stake center. Don't bother with church clothes—the meeting will be in the parking lot. Too dark inside."

What could that be about? I wondered while we tried to keep ourselves busy until the specified time.

Time dragged while we waited, but when the assigned hour finally came, the boys hopped into the back of the Bluebird, and with Mom and me in the cab, we drove to the Yakima stake center. I looked around anxiously while we drove into town. A few people milled around, but this was not the Yakima I knew. I saw no sign of electricity. The stores looked locked up tight, the marquees that used to flash and scroll messages hung dark and mute, and the traffic lights weren't working.

I could guess what was passing through the local shopkeepers' minds. They must be frantic with worry about losing their businesses and not just because there were no customers. Some people might think no power meant "help yourself to our stock." We passed a shop that already had boards nailed over its windows, a preemptive strike against future looters. Looters in Yakima! Well, maybe it could happen.

We passed a few more boarded-up shops, and I wondered if they knew something we didn't. After all, we'd been isolated from any kind of news, except that one radio message. What was really going on?

The parking lot of the stake center was jammed with cars and trucks, in contrast to the rest of the quiet town. People hung around the vehicles, talking in clusters. The rest of Yakima had to be wondering what the Mormons were up to.

As soon as we stepped from the truck, voices surrounded us, filling our ears with impossibility. I reeled, a wave of shock cresting over me.

". . . the grid is down all over the West . . . maybe farther . . . bombs . . ."

"Martial law . . . transportation completely down . . . chaos in the big cities . . ."

No, no, no. This cannot be happening. Not now. Not when Dad isn't here.

Dad would make everything all right, if only he were here.

The four of us stood together in an odd little huddle. I looked at Mom, Jarron, and Ethan, seeing my own fear reflected back in their wide eyes.

Was Dad all right, wherever he was?

"It's okay, it's okay, it's okay," Mom said over and over, like a mantra.

I swallowed hard. What would happen? I said a quick prayer of thanks that we lived in a relatively obscure corner of the country. But I felt scared right down to my bones. I wanted to cover my ears, block out the terrifying tales floating in and out and around.

Behind me, I heard the gruff voice of Brother Gibson from our ward. "The first thing I put in my food storage was ammunition." I looked over my shoulder at him, and sure enough, he stood Rambo-like, a hunting rifle resting across his arms. "I'm not going anywhere without my gun until this is over." The men around him nodded agreement.

I shivered.

"Look!" Ethan pointed to a jacked-up pickup in the middle of the parking lot. Two men helped our stake president, President Green, into the back. The two men climbed in after him, and I recognized them as his counselors. Obviously, the truck would serve as his speaking platform.

Finally, a legitimate reason for a lift kit.

Someone leaned into the truck through the window and laid on the horn, long and loud. A shocked hush fell over the crowd.

A man handed President Green a battery-powered megaphone. Everyone in the crowd turned expectantly toward him, each standing by or sitting on their own vehicles.

"Sorta reminds me of King Benjamin," I whispered to Jarron.

He grinned.

President Green had an imposing presence. Not physically, exactly, being neither short nor tall. But I'd always thought his thick white hair—not even beginning to thin—and high, angular cheekbones gave him the look of an apostle. Why I thought that, I didn't know, since most of the current apostles had very little hair. I guess he looked David O. McKay–ish or something. But it was more than that. He seemed to have an intensely spiritual aura, something I could feel, even from this distance.

"Brothers and sisters, may I have your attention," President Green said into the megaphone.

I held my breath. What would he say next? At that moment, I wouldn't have been surprised if he'd said the moon was scheduled to turn to blood next Tuesday night.

"As you know, alarming events are unfolding. People are scared and confused. Life as we have known it will never be the same, it seems."

I stole a glance at Mom and my brothers. Their eyes were riveted on President Green's face.

"What I want to say may be hard for you to hear," he continued. "What I am going to ask of you will not be easy. But I want you to know I say it under inspiration."

Even the children were silent. The moment brimmed with significance.

"The government of our land—that we have always depended on for peace and safety—is in disarray. I am sorry to tell you, if you have not already heard, that a terrorist bomb destroyed the US capital, killing more than half of Congress and the president. Other well-timed attacks have disabled the power grid, and our dear land is plunged into chaos. Martial law has been declared, and the military is struggling at this moment to regain control of the large cities in America.

"Their hope is that they will soon be able to right things and that the transportation of food and necessities will resume soon. But I have had communication with Church headquarters. The leaders there feel it may be a long time before things are settled. We will have to be self-reliant and not depend on the government."

Panic rose in my throat. I felt Mom's fingernails dig into my arm.

"The worst has not happened. Hanford wasn't hit with a nuclear attack, as far as I know," President Green continued. "It did sustain damage of some kind, and containment of its waste storage is in question. Because of this danger and our isolation from food supplies, the Church has called a few stakes to gather to Utah. The Yakima Stake is one of them."

I caught my breath as a murmur swept the crowd. Gather to Utah? What did he mean by that?

President Green's face remained calm as he held up a reassuring hand. "This will be the greatest challenge our stake has faced. We must heed this call and travel to Utah, where we will be kept under the Church's protective arm. There, the Church's vast resources will be used to care for us until further plans can be made. I recognize the difficulty of what I'm asking you, but we will leave this valley in three days."

The crowd erupted in shocked exclamations. One man shouted, "I ain't goin' nowhere. I don't care what anyone says. You'll have to drag me outta here." I heard a few words of agreement here and there in the crowd.

The horn honked again, and the crowd fell silent as President Green once more held up a hand. "My dear brothers and sisters, I know this is hard. We'll all have to help each other. No one is going to force you to come with us. But I ask you with all my heart to do so. I firmly believe it's no longer safe to stay here. Now then, I will give you a few instructions. Please listen carefully. This will be a huge undertaking, but a system of organization is already in place with our quorums and wards. Your first task will be to report to your bishop the number of gallons of gasoline you have on your respective ranches. I hope those of you with tanks will remain the generous Christian souls I know you to be and realize we'll need to pool our resources to move such a large group so fast. Please give him this number, along with the number of fifty-five gallon drums you might have and types of vehicles you own before you leave this meeting.

"Secondly, as soon as you get home today, begin gathering the food storage you have so faithfully put away. Pack the vehicle you plan to use with enough to sustain your own family for two weeks, and take the rest to your ward building. If you have need, the bishops will redistribute to you. If there is more than enough, we will leave it behind for the people who remain in this area. Two weeks' worth will be more than enough to see us safely into the hands of the Church in Utah. I feel confident we have enough fuel and food to take us the seven hundred or so miles. Shouldn't take more than twelve hours."

At this point, at least two men turned from their places and left the parking lot. What were they doing?

"After you've packed your two weeks' worth of food, choose carefully among your clothing and other necessities. Don't forget medicines you need. I know this will be very hard, but obviously, you can't bring everything. I'm sorry to tell you I don't know if we'll be able to return. Be prayerful as you do this, and realize your families are really the only possessions that matter in the long run.

"I know you have a hundred questions. Utilize the chains of organization already in place and direct questions to your bishopric and quorum leaders. Report back here, ready to leave, on Friday morning. God bless you in your efforts to prepare."

President Green handed the megaphone to one of his counselors, who offered a prayer. After the amen, they climbed off the truck bed. The parking lot surged with a roar of noise. I saw a few people crying, and not just women. Three or four cars drove off immediately, but most of the crowd stayed put as people sought each other out for opinions and reassurance.

"Hang on a second. I'll be right back," I said to Mom and the boys. I plunged into the mass of people, aiming for President Green's white head, which I could still see near the podium truck. Thankfully, I didn't get jostled too much—I guess the sight of my cane prompted people to let me through.

Even though President Green had asked that people save questions for their respective bishops, quite a few still vied for his attention. I wasn't surprised. After all, I was doing the same thing. I stood at the edge of the group and waited while he patiently deflected each person, some to their ward officials, some to his counselors. Before too long, he caught my eye, and I was surprised to see his face light with recognition. I didn't think he knew me—I'd never talked to him in person before.

He held a hand out to me, the same one he'd reassured the crowd with. I took it, and he gently pulled me through the press of people.

"Sister Hatch, how are you?" He smiled at me, his face crinkling.

"Fine," I stammered. "But I did want to ask you—if you don't mind— if you know anything about my dad. The bishop doesn't know when he will be back—we haven't heard from him—we don't even know where he is—and now this—" I cleared my throat to stop my voice from catching.

"I've been thinking about you and your family," he replied.

I stared in amazement. He'd thought about us? With all that was going on?

"This has been difficult for you Hatches. I recognize that. But you'll be with your dad soon, God willing. We're aware of your situation—that you'll have to make this trip without your dad. But don't worry. We'll watch out for you and for others who need help. And Amélie"—he stooped a little so he could look directly into my eyes—"you've got some mettle in you. You'll be fine." He squeezed my arm and turned into the throng.

"But President . . ." My voice disappeared in the clamor.

I stared at his retreating form as the crowd closed in front of him. I couldn't grasp what I had heard in the last hour. The government in chaos? Leave our home? Mettle in me? I didn't feel strong at all. Grateful for my cane, I struggled back to the waiting Bluebird. Mom gave the bishop our fuel estimate, and we drove back home.

That evening, the boys went out to move the sprinklers as usual, but I had to wonder, what was the point? If in three days we picked up and left, the fields certainly wouldn't get watered again. Would someone else take over our crops? Should I care?

Mom and I started sorting through the food storage. A great deal of it would be of no use to us. Sacks of wheat and beans? Powdered milk? Instant potatoes? We couldn't eat that stuff on a trip to Utah. And how long could we eat canned chili and fruit cocktail before we got sick of it—or just plain sick?

Mom didn't react when I told her about my conversation with President Green. Her hands kept moving, stacking cans and boxes and loading jars into cases.

I couldn't stop thinking about Zack. What would happen to him and his dad? No doubt they would think we were a bunch of lunatics. Maybe they would be the ones to farm our land. I wouldn't mind that, but I'd rather they were safe. And no matter how crazy it sounded, I believed President Green. He knew. It wasn't safe here.

While we worked, I focused my mind. *Zack. Zack. Zack.* Maybe he'd feel my thoughts somehow and come over and talk to me. I might be a lunatic Mormon, but I wasn't crazy enough to walk over to his house in the dark. That was a recurring nightmare of mine . . . I'd trip, fall, and not be able to get up . . . I'd lie there all night . . .

At ten o'clock, I gave up and went to bed. Zack would have to wait until morning to hear what the crazy Mormons were doing. Maybe by then the whole county would know.

Somewhere around two or three in the morning, I woke up to the dog barking his fool head off. I groaned and pulled the quilts over my head. "Stop with the barking, Buddy," I muttered into my pillow.

My thoughts wandered to what we'd do with Buddy when we left. Then his barking stopped abruptly, sort of midbark. Weird. I lay there under the quilts for a moment, listening. Quiet pervaded the farm but then . . . Did I hear a faint voice? A clink of metal on metal?

Maybe one of the boys went out to hush the dog, I thought. I walked to my window and parted the curtains, looking out across the yard toward the barn. Moonlight slanted through the trees, and in its light, I saw a large, unfamiliar form huddled by the far side of the barn.

I blinked, trying to clear the sleep from my eyes. What was that? I squinted, and fear struck hard. A truck. Two men walked with careful steps around it; another sat barely visible in the cab. What were they doing?

My heart thudded. I knew exactly what they were doing. Pumping gas out of our tank into a large container in the back of the truck. Stealing our gas!

CHAPTER FIVE

Tuesday, May 22

RAGE AND FEAR SWEPT OVER me. What would happen to us now? How could we travel to Utah without gas? Somehow I had to stop them.

Opening the window and shouting at them would do no good. What could I do—one girl with a bum leg. I couldn't call the police. Even if the phones weren't down, they'd never get here in time. There wasn't even time to send someone running to Zack's house. What would Dad do?

I thought of the guns in Dad's closet—a hunting rifle, a shotgun, and a pistol. They sat in a long plastic tub on the top shelf, along with several boxes of ammunition. Dad used to hunt a lot but hadn't as much recently, so the guns came out of the closet only occasionally. He'd had me practice with them a couple of times, but I'd never touched them without him. The thought of using one made my insides squirm.

I could shoot into the air and scare them off, I thought. I could do that. Or maybe I could shoot their tires and keep them from getting away with the gas.

I stood there trying to galvanize myself into activity. I pictured going into my parents' bedroom, entering the closet, finding something to stand on, wrestling the plastic tub down, choosing which gun, loading it, dealing with my mom, who would certainly wake up and would certainly freak out, going outside, and bravely shooting air or tires or maybe even legs. These thoughts dashed through my mind in an instant. I steeled myself and turned.

The sound of a motor starting drew me back to the window. The truck pulled away, laden with our gas. It was too late.

* * *

In the morning, before I even told Mom about the gas, I set out for Zack's. I really, really needed to talk to Zack. I considered sending one of the boys to go get him, but it seemed a bit dramatic. After all, I could walk. Not fast, but I could walk.

When I went outside, I found that what I'd dreaded was true. They'd killed Buddy. His body lay stiff and cold beside the gas tank. Everyone would freak when they found out, and Ethan would have to bury him.

When I approached, Zack and his dad were in the field just west of their house, wrangling some sprinkler pipe. As soon as Zack saw me, he dropped the pipe and hurried over.

"Hey," he said, a bit breathless. "You okay?"

"Yeah, but something's happened. Actually, sort of a lot is happening. D'you have a minute?" I glanced at Mr. Allman.

Zack waved at his dad and held up an index finger. "I was going to come over as soon as I got done with this. We heard some crazy stuff—is it true? I mean . . . about the Mormons?"

I bit my lip. I wanted to let it all spill out and listen to Zack tell me everything was going to be okay. But I had to think it through and say it right, say it so Zack wouldn't think it was "crazy stuff" . . . say it so Zack would believe it.

"Well, yes, if you mean the Mormons are packing up and leaving." I peered sideways at Zack, anxious for his reaction. "Listen, Zack. Stuff is happening that makes it too dangerous to stay." I put my hand on his arm. "I know it sounds crazy. But our leaders—they know stuff. Zack—come with us. You and your dad both."

Zack's eyes flew wide. "What? You're leaving? For real? This trouble's going to end right away; you'll see. Your crops, your land, your home!" Zack looked into my eyes. I felt them search me inside and out. "Are the Mormon leaders making you do this? Do you have to? Or they'll throw you out of your church or something?"

"No, it's not like that. They really do know it's best to leave. And Zack—I believe them. There's radiation leaking from Hanford, and they have information about supplies and stuff being cut off. Please, Zack. Think about it. You could come with us—and be safe."

"Amélie," Zack said, gentling his voice. I looked up at him, my heart in my throat. Zack never called me by my real name. "You have to know Dad would never leave. Especially not with the Mormons."

"Promise you'll at least try?" I asked. "Tell him it's just a way of getting out of here with a large, safe group. It's not like you'd have to get baptized a Mormon or something. I'd make sure no one hassled you."

Zack shook his head ruefully, pursing his lips. Then a big grin spread across his face.

"What?" I demanded.

"I just got a mental image of you protecting me against the big bad baptizers." He curled his arms like a bodybuilder and snickered.

I found it necessary to whack him with my cane. "I'm serious, Zack."

"I'll let Dad know what you've said, but I can't think of anything he's less likely to do. Are you pretty set on going? If it's because your dad's gone, you know we'll look out for you here."

"Yeah, we gotta go." I bit my lip again. "There's just one snag. Last night, some guys came and stole all the gas out of our tank. Killed Buddy too."

"What?" Zack almost screeched. "Who?"

"I have no idea. It was dark. But just the day before, everyone reported to their bishops how much gas they had."

"So you think the bishops had something to do with it?" Zack's voice was incredulous.

"No. No way. I mean, if you knew our bishop . . ." My voice trailed away. I wondered if anyone else's gas had been bothered. "But someone else, someone bad, must have seen that list."

Zack looked quizzically at me.

"Talk to him," I repeated. "Use all your superpower persuasiveness."

"Holy cow, Lee. How am I supposed to talk him into something I don't even know is a good idea?"

I thrust my face close to his. "Zack! Radiation! Starvation!"

He laughed and put up his hands. "Okay, okay, I'll pass along your message. I better get back." He motioned with his head to where Mr. Allman still stood, waiting.

"Will you come and tell me what he says? Later, after chores?"

"Sure."

As I walked home, I wondered if any other ward members had had midnight visitors or if any non-Mormons had.

Dad, I could've used you about now. I was tired of trying to be smart and brave. I wanted him to come take over, make all the decisions. I wanted him to tell me it didn't matter that all of our gas was stolen. I wanted him to tell me that going to Utah was the right thing. I mostly wanted him to just be there and tell me he loved me and that we were still a family.

* * *

I was right. Mom did freak out, and this time when she marched out with the keys to the Bluebird, bent on visiting the bishop, nothing stopped her. I couldn't tell what the boys thought. They didn't say a word as I described what happened. Ethan just nodded when I asked him to bury Buddy. When he was finished, the three of us sat in the living room, saying absolutely nothing until Mom got back.

When Mom got home, she flung herself onto the couch beside me. She looked rattled . . . even more than usual. The bishop had definitely shaken her cage. The boys and me just watched and waited until she could speak.

"Let's see . . . where to start," she finally said. "The bishop said he was really sorry about our gas, but we weren't the only ones. Nearly everyone who had tanks got hit. And even some people not in the Church, just for good measure, I guess."

"But what's going to happen?" I asked in a rush. "There won't be enough gas for everyone now."

"That's right. They're forming a plan now, but it looks like there is only enough gas for some big trucks, which will haul supplies. The people will have to get to Utah under their own power."

"What does that mean? There's *nowhere* else we can get gas."

Mom's lips turned in a tremulous smile. "What that means, babies, is . . . we are going to walk to Utah."

"What?" Ethan screeched. "What do you mean, *walk?*"

I couldn't speak. Mom could not have meant what it sounded like she said.

"I know, I know," Mom said, her hands fluttering in the air in front of her face. I gaped at her. Surely she had misunderstood the bishop.

"That's impossible," Jarron said. "What do I look like, a freakin' pioneer?"

"See for yourself." Mom thrust a scrap of paper into my hands. "The bishop wrote down some instructions for us."

I felt too scared to even look at the paper. *Walk?* I forced my eyes to the bishop's scribblings.

Everyone was still supposed to meet at the stake center on Friday as planned. But now each person was to pack only two changes of clothing into a backpack, along with any personal items, like eyeglasses or medicine, and a water bottle. Nothing else. Anything we brought would have to be carried.

Tomorrow we were to bring our food storage and camping gear to the stake center, and some lucky people would try to pack two big cargo trucks with the right combination of food, water, and sleeping supplies for the whole stake.

Six hundred sixty miles. In seminary I'd learned that in pioneer times, twenty miles was considered a good day's travel. I guessed we'd be lucky to do half that much, seeing as how we were all a bunch of soft, lazy modern people, to say nothing of the elderly—and handicapped. So this would take somewhere around two months.

Even if I had two good legs, I couldn't imagine doing this.

"Mom, please tell me you talked to the bishop about Dad. Please tell me he's just around the corner." I fought to keep my voice steady.

"I did talk to him about Dad." Mom fidgeted with her hair and bit her bottom lip. We waited. Mom opened and closed her mouth a couple of times.

"What?" I demanded. "Tell us what he said."

"Ummm . . ."

"That's it. I'm going over there myself." I pushed myself off the couch.

"No, no, wait," Mom said, her hands catching at my clothes. "The bishop did tell me where Dad is. He's fine. He's okay. He's doing some stuff for the Church. The bishop said we could be real proud of him and of what he's doing."

I put my hands on my hips. "So where is he?"

"Can't say. Not yet."

"You're not going to tell us?"

"He made me swear I wouldn't tell anyone, not even you three. Don't worry. He's safe."

"So we're supposed to be okay with that? Just walk to Utah. No big deal. Us, alone, no Dad. Walk."

"Yes. And we can do it," Mom said. I was pretty sure she was talking herself into it as well as us.

I went to my room and lay down on my bed. I stared up at the water spot on the ceiling and forced my hands to be still, keeping them from drumming by my sides.

Was this it, then? Not just the last days, like they always said at church, but the very last days? I'd pictured it differently. Where were the Four Horsemen of the Apocalypse and those people who wanted to brand me with *666* on my forehead? What about the earthquake du jour and streets running with blood? My room looked just as it always had, with the afternoon sun filtering through the lace cutwork on the curtains my grandmother had made. She had been born too late to be a pioneer.

Mettle in me, President Green had said. Well, where was it? I only felt weak and scared. I imagined myself making the whole stake annoyed as they waited for me to hobble along. Or me way behind them all. Way way behind.

I should pray. I rolled onto my stomach and pulled my legs up under me so I sort of knelt, stink-bug style.

"Heavenly Father . . ." I hoped God wouldn't mind if I skipped the protocol and got straight to the asking-for-stuff part. "Bless me that I'll be able to handle whatever comes." I couldn't help shivering a little, contemplating that big unknown whatever. I started rattling off my rote list of people to bless: my brothers, my mom . . . oh yes, Mom. I poured my heart into that moment of prayer. She would need every bit of divine help she could get.

And Dad. Wherever he was, off on his super-secret, super-important mission. Even more super-important than being with us.

That started making me grouchy, so I said a hasty amen.

I waited until the sun went down for Zack to come over, but he didn't show. Things must have gotten busy at the Allman place. Chores were certainly different without power. And without gas for the wheel lines, we couldn't water anymore. The boys rotated the hand lines as much as they could, but we didn't have enough of those to water everything. The Allmans would be in the same situation.

But what did it matter if our crops didn't get enough water? We'd leave them in only a few days, and we wouldn't be back in time to save them. Maybe never.

In the morning, we started loading the Bluebird with our food storage. Thank goodness for brothers—they lugged stuff out of the basement for what seemed like hours, while Mom and I arranged the collection in the bed of the truck. Sacks and sacks and sacks of grain, oats, flour, and sugar, and cases upon cases of canned stuff. Mom might not have been the typical Mormon mom, but she took her food storage seriously.

Zack still hadn't come over by late afternoon, so I set off for their place. But no one was around, and their truck wasn't in the driveway. They must have gone to town, although I couldn't think why. No stores were open. I walked back home, trying not to be annoyed.

* * *

I took my biology and world civ textbooks out of my backpack, tossed them in the corner, and dumped the remaining pile of papers over the trashcan without even looking through them.

Deep breath. What would I pack? What still had meaning in a world with no school, no electricity, no home? Would I ever again see the things we'd leave behind?

I looked at the stuff littering the top of my dresser. On the left lay a folder from the school counselor containing ACT test grades and college brochures. Definitely wouldn't need that. Nail polish? No way. Jewelry? I sifted through the tangle of necklaces and earrings but, in the end, left them where they lay. I picked up a sketchbook with a few horrid attempts at drawing inside and flung that in the corner with the books.

My scriptures and the little Moleskine notebook I used as a journal . . . okay, those, at least, were for sure. I tucked them in the bottom of the backpack.

My fingers trailed regretfully over a pile of piano books, tossed there after my last lesson. I hadn't practiced a lick since the power went off. When would I play again? I knew I couldn't carry them, but I could scarcely make myself put them aside. They'd have piano books in Utah.

My iPod lay there, the headphones hanging down over the drawer handles. I picked it up hopefully. Had I charged it? I popped the buds into my ears and pressed play.

Nothing happened. Drat.

Next to it were a couple of CDs I'd burned. The top one was labeled "Real Emotion." I couldn't help humming the tune that sprang to my mind.

Tell it to me straight—I can take it
Don't pretend, and please don't fake it . . .

Ryan Cook! I laughed out loud. I didn't even remember burning that. I thought of the last time I'd seen him and how angry he'd made me. Well, how angry at myself he'd made me. I could picture him as the song played in my mind, his messy dark curls flopping over his eyes as he tossed his head . . .

I forced the song out, replacing it with Brahms. Much better.

Two changes of clothing, the instructions said. I took two pairs of jeans out of a drawer and stuffed them in the pack, along with a T-shirt, a long-sleeve, button-up shirt, and a hoodie. I tucked a few pairs of underwear and socks along the sides. *At least I don't have to wear petticoats*, I thought. That'd be all I'd need. I pictured trying to hike up some rocky hillside in a long skirt with my bum leg and a cane.

The pack already bulged. Well, that made decisions simple. I'd be lucky to get a toothbrush in there.

Mom and the boys were about done too. Packing was no big deal when you could only take one small backpack. Tomorrow morning we'd close up this house and leave everything behind. What would happen? Would the stuff sit here awaiting our return, or would looters get to it? The thought of people breaking in and messing with our belongings made my skin crawl.

Stepping outside, I looked toward Zack's house. Some things felt harder to leave behind than others. When I asked him to come with us, I knew there wasn't a chance. But leaving my oldest friend in a place that was no longer safe felt like a stab.

I stumped off down the gravel drive toward his house. Dratted boy. I spent half my days dragging my sorry self over to talk to him, it seemed. Still, I couldn't leave without saying good-bye.

How would I do it? I'd always had Zack around. I couldn't imagine life without him. All the photos, pianos, iPods, and clothes in the world were a hundred times easier to walk away from than him.

When I got to Zack's place, my eyes went straight for their truck's parking spot out front. Still missing. How odd! Had the Allmans come home and left again, or were they still away? That seemed impossible. I gazed across their fields, looking for the truck on a canal road or something, but I couldn't see it anywhere. Well, maybe one of them was home. I knocked on the side door and stepped inside, as was our custom.

"Zack? Mr. Allman?" The house looked dark and quiet.

"Lee?" Zack's voice floated from around the corner. "Is that you?" He sounded strained.

I followed his voice to the front room. Zack sat on the sofa, his arms resting on his knees. With only a small window, the room was full of shadows.

"Whatcha doin', Zack, sitting here in the dark?" I sat down beside him. Now close, I could see something was wrong. Something was very, very wrong. My eyes darted over him. He didn't look hurt, but his face had the look of someone who fought with all they had to keep it together.

Zack opened his mouth but then just cleared his throat. He closed his eyes.

"What's happened?" I asked. Fear leaped up in my throat.

I waited. Zack said nothing but made a heartrending, strangled little sound.

"Lee-Lee," he whispered. "They killed him. They killed my dad."

"What?" Horror struck my heart. "Who?"

"I don't know. A gang. They just wanted the truck. That's all. They just wanted the truck." Zack looked at me, his face sagging with misery. "They shot him and dragged him out of it, left him. Right out front."

"No!" Tears sprang to my eyes. "Oh, Zack! When? I came over yesterday afternoon and—thought you went to town—the truck was gone—"

"Must've been right before that. Yesterday. I'm glad you didn't come when they were here."

Struggling to find words, I put my arms around him, and he hugged me back. I could feel his jerky swallows, the way people do when they're trying not to cry. Finally he let go, wiping his eyes with his shirtsleeve.

"But why? That old truck? It's nearly as bad as the Bluebird," I said, my voice quavering.

"Dad told me just that morning he'd heard there'd been something called an electromagnetic pulse, an EMP, he'd said. Some terrorists set it off, exploded it in the atmosphere or something. It's a thing that disables computers, any kind, big or small. And all the cars nowadays have computers in them—"

"But your truck is too old to have a computer. So it would be one of the only vehicles left around that'll still run," I broke in. "And you've been here by yourself since—since it happened? Why didn't you come over?"

"I've . . . been busy," he mumbled. "Had to . . ." Zack gulped. "Had to build a box. Had to bury him."

I stared at him wordlessly, stroking his arm.

"And Lee-Lee, there's something else," Zack said to the floor. "I think I . . . I'm sure I killed one of them. I fired at them. I broke the windshield, and I saw one of them . . . lots of blood . . . they drove away . . ."

My stomach clenched. Sobs choked my throat.

"Zack!" I croaked. He hugged me again, and this time his embrace crushed me against him. I felt his chest heave with spasms of weeping.

"Take me with you," he said.

Chapter Six

A SOMBER GROUP LEFT OUR place the next morning. Mom and the boys rode in the cab. Zack and I sat in the truck bed with all of the backpacks.

I brushed away tears as the house and farm faded from view, but my pitiful thoughts swallowed up when I looked at Zack. He huddled next to me against the cab window, his face ashen, his eyes downcast. He'd spoken only a few grim words of greeting to Mom and the boys, nothing else. I'd told them about Mr. Allman. And of course they'd said Zack should come with us.

When we pulled onto the highway, the speed whipped my hair in stinging lashes across my face. As I brought my hand up to gather my hair away from my eyes, it brushed against Zack's jacket, pulling it aside. I saw he wore a pistol in a holster under his arm.

Zack followed my gaze. "The new me, I suppose." His voice was barely discernible above the roar of road noise. He shrugged and looked at his feet again.

The truck sped down the deserted road. As we neared Yakima, other vehicles joined ours on the road, many headed to the stake center as we were. All looked old—none new enough to be affected by the electromagnetic pulse. On the outskirts of the city, a family I recognized from the stake walked along the side of the road toward town. I knocked on the window and motioned to Mom. She pulled over.

"Hey!" I beckoned with a hand as we pulled up beside the family. "Come on." The group eagerly climbed over the tailgate. The scene repeated itself as we got closer to the stake center, and by the time we got there, people and packs completely stuffed the Bluebird's bed.

We joined a line of vehicles waiting to pull into the parking lot, and people on foot streamed in around us. When our turn came, a man in the stake high council approached Mom's window with a clipboard. I scooted near so I could listen in.

"Hello, Sister Hatch," he said. "Lucky this thing's running. We'll need it."

Mom nodded, her eyes wide. "Sure. Whatever."

"First, how many gallons of gas do you estimate are in your truck?"

Mom checked the gauge. "I'd guess fifteen or so. I don't know."

The high councilor scribbled on his clipboard. "Pull right over there." He motioned to a corner of the parking lot. "That's where the Zillah Ward is gathering. Bishop Taylor will give you instructions."

A high degree of order emerged from the apparent chaos of the parking lot. Each of the ten wards had its own designated area. Large cargo trucks stacked with food and supplies crowded the center of the parking lot, along with a huge water tanker. Several horse trailers angled to the side, and a few people held horses. The sound of hundreds of people talking filled the air.

We made our way to the Zillah corner and got out of the truck, and the others who rode in with us drifted off to their own wards. Bishop Taylor walked over and shook our hands.

"And you are?" he asked when he came to Zack. I opened my mouth, but Zack spoke first.

"Zack Allman. I'm a neighbor of the Hatches."

"That's fine, son. Everyone just make yourselves comfy for now. When a few more people get here, I'll give the instructions."

A couple hundred people milled about our area. I recognized most of the active folks from the ward. The parents looked resigned, waiting patiently for someone to tell them what to do. Kids ran about, excited about the promise of adventure.

A half hour later, Bishop Taylor raised a hand. "Okay, we're going to go ahead and get started. First, an opening prayer seems in order. Brother Andelin? Would you?"

Brother Andelin, a thin, older fellow with bristly black hair, bowed his head.

Seems like people always pray that we'll travel in safety, but never did those words hold so much meaning. At least I could hear his voice over the hubbub of the other wards around us.

I peered through my eyelashes at Zack. What would he think of our style of praying? He stood stiffly, arms at his sides. I thought how odd it must look to him that Mormons folded their arms across their chest. I'd grown up with it, so it seemed normal to me, but what would he think about it?

Zack showed no expression. At least he didn't make the sign of the cross at the amen.

"Here's the plan," Bishop Taylor said. "We've added up how much gas we have. The supply trucks are carrying enough to get them to Utah. The amount we have left has been divided between the other vehicles. If we make several trips, we can ferry everyone to our first rendezvous point in Sunnyside. We'll spend our first night there, and then we'll have to leave the other vehicles behind. It's an hour and a half round trip, and we've got hundreds of people to ferry, so get cozy. Some folks won't be leaving Yakima until late."

"Where will we camp?" one brother asked.

"In the Sunnyside Ward chapel."

Of course! I thought. Indoors, bathrooms, and a kitchen set up to feed a crowd, even if there was no electricity.

"We're going to split the ward into groups of hundreds, fifties, and tens—like the old days." Bishop Taylor smiled through the worry lines etched on his face. "It seemed to work well then. We have roughly two hundred people from our ward here, so my counselors will captain one hundred each. The elders and high priests quorum leaders will form the fifties and tens. Hang around this area until we get everything settled. We'll tell you which group you're in and in which order you'll be leaving for Sunnyside."

Zack sat down on the bumper of the Bluebird and folded his arms. I hurried to sit beside him. "I shouldn't be here," he said. "This is nuts."

"Absolutely you should. It's not safe to stay."

Zack's face darkened, and I cringed. Who knew better than Zack about how safe it was around here? Why couldn't I learn to think before speaking?

"I gotta talk to your priest or whatever you call him." Zack stood and strode toward Bishop Taylor. I scurried after him.

"Excuse me, sir," Zack said, standing at the bishop's elbow.

"Hello, son."

"Um, well, I thought you should know before you get things all set up that I'm not a Mormon."

Bishop Taylor put a hand on Zack's shoulder. "Oh, I know, son. That's fine. You're welcome to come with us. Anyone is."

"Are there others . . . ?"

"A few. Not many. Not as many members as we'd hoped either. But we're not going to force anyone. Don't worry. If it makes you feel better, I appreciate you being here with the Hatches, seeing as how they're without their dad and all." Bishop Taylor smiled and turned to peer at a clipboard someone held out to him.

Zack shook his head and went back to the Bluebird. He looked lost and a little wild-eyed, like a trapped animal. I tried to talk to him, but it was like speaking to a statue.

Zack has to go with us, I thought. He can't change his mind, not now! As the hours ticked past, he looked alternately like he was resigned to his fate and then about to bolt.

Finally, it was our turn to leave. This was the moment. They assigned us to the group Brother Dowding of the high priests quorum headed, and we ended up going in the Bluebird. This time the whole family was in the back, along with nine others. It looked like a clown car. Zack finally climbed in.

The highway was deserted except for us and another carload from our group—not that there was a lot of traffic between Yakima and Sunnyside even on a normal day. The eerie quiet intensified when we drove into Sunnyside. Only a few people, and no cars, wandered the streets.

But inside the church, the noise hummed through the halls. Men pulled out tables and chairs from their places under the stage and set them up in the gym. Clearly, we'd have to eat in stages, with a whole stake descending on this little building. Women clogged the kitchen, bustling about, opening cans of veggies and pouring them into big pots. Others opened package after package of meat, creating piles of styrofoam trays and freezer paper. At least this church had gas stoves. Things would undoubtedly change down the road.

"Hey, boys," Brother Dowding motioned to Zack, Ethan, and Jarron. "Give us a hand with this bedding?" Soon they became part of a train of hands, passing bedding from the trucks to the stage, where it was being stacked. I watched Zack, hoping to see him perk up at being included. But I couldn't read the expression on his face, although I thought I knew him better than I knew my own brothers.

I looked at the people around me, the church becoming ever more crowded as carloads continued to arrive. Most of the faces looked familiar—I'd seen them for years at stake conferences, although I didn't know all their names, especially outside the Zillah Ward. I did know the kids my age though. We had frequent stake dances where we'd see kids from neighboring high schools. And there was a sort of Mormon radar in operation, forming the acceptable dating pool. Not that I dated.

Why was that? I didn't think I was hopelessly ugly. I suppose I considered myself average looking, with the typical teenager long hair and run-of-the-mill brown eyes. Was it the leg? Perhaps. Or maybe I was a little odd, to match my name. Besides, who'd want to take a cripple girl to a dance?

I wandered into the gym, where quite a few people sat at the tables, talking and watching the children scamper. They didn't sit there because they were so anxious to be fed—there was just nowhere else to hang out. I noticed Mom giving another lady a neck massage, the two of them in deep conversation. No doubt Mom was analyzing the lady's dreams or giving her some feng shui tips. I smiled.

My eyes did a double take. There, in the corner, in a group of newly arrived people, his back toward me, stood a young man with a head of dark curls, and he was holding a guitar case. It couldn't be anyone else.

Ryan Cook.

I crossed the room, my cane tapping on the wooden gym floor. "Ryan!" My voice sliced across the noise of conversation.

Ryan looked over his shoulder and grinned when he saw me. He parted the sea of people clustered around him and closed the distance between us with long strides.

"Well! Hi there, secretary."

"What are you doing here?" I demanded. It was perfectly right and good for Zack to be with us, but Ryan? That was pushing it. Although I couldn't say why.

Ryan put on an offended look. "Why shouldn't I be?" He put the guitar case down and set his slender fingers on the hips of his jeans.

"I mean . . . how did you . . . You're . . ." I stammered, my cheeks heating.

"You mean why am I here with a bunch of crazy Mormons who think they're going to walk all the way to Utah? Haven't you got room for a celebrity like yours truly?"

"I'm surprised you'd consider being seen with us crazy Mormons."

"Seemed like the thing to do. I fancy myself a traveling minstrel now. Besides, I'm a Mormon. I suppose I've got just as much right to be here as you. For all I know, you're the Gentile. You never told me you were a Mormon."

My mouth gaped like a fish. "You? Mormon? Liar. I've never seen you at stake conference or anything."

"I didn't say I was gung ho. But yes, I'm an honest-to-goodness member, thoroughly baptized as a kid."

"I don't believe it," I said more to myself than to him and shook my head.

"Don't be like that." He put an arm around my shoulders. "We've got a long trip ahead of us. Might as well be friends." He smiled, and my insides flip-flopped. I couldn't help myself.

"Sure." I smiled back. "What about the rest of your band?"

"They're the Gentiles." He grinned.

A difficult job is nothing but a challenge for Mormons, it seemed. The kitchen ladies cooked and served the gigantic meal with few problems, considering what they had to work with. There were a few jokes about feeding the five thousand and good-natured ribbing about the mostly meat meal being a Word of Wisdom infraction. But there was a lot of meat that needed to be used while still fresh, and Mormons hate to waste stuff. So we ate a lot, keeping in mind there could be times in the future there wouldn't be as much. Coolers would keep things for a couple of days but not for long.

Then began the colossal undertaking of getting everyone bedded down for the night. The guys put away the tables and chairs and quickly mopped the gym floor, which soon resembled a patchwork quilt, with sleeping bags laid as closely as possible. Moms and babies were assigned classrooms where they could cry each other to sleep. People lay their heads on every bench in the chapel, kids curling up underneath just like they do in sacrament meeting.

People stuffed into every nook and cranny. Mom, Ethan, Jarron, Zack, and I ended up in the Primary room, smashed between the piano and the pulpit. I wondered if the cramped quarters would inhibit the younger ones from sleeping, but I guess the angels watched over us because the kids throughout the building settled down pretty well in spite of their strange surroundings. I suppose the fact the church was dark helped; there were only a few battery-powered lanterns placed strategically throughout the building and just one in the Primary room. Without light, there wasn't much else to do except sleep.

I watched Zack with one eye as our Primary room group knelt on our bedrolls and prayed together. A sweet spirit settled over us, and I wondered if he could feel it. He didn't say anything as he crawled into his bag between Ethan and Jarron.

Sometime in the early morning, I felt a touch on my shoulder. I woke with a start to see the dark shape of a man squatting beside me.

"Sister Hatch, it's okay. It's me, Bishop Taylor."

I sat up, rubbing my sleepy eyes. "Is something wrong, Bishop?"

"No, everything's fine. The stake president has asked you to come to the chapel and play some hymns on the organ."

"Huh?"

"You know, as a wake-up. Reveille. We want to get moving and out of here soon. Folks are already getting food ready."

I couldn't help a little laugh. "Okay. I guess I can do that."

I stepped over sleeping bodies and slowly threaded my way to the chapel. Only a glimmer of light slanted through the tall windows at the sides of the stand and the funeral doors, so I picked up a lantern at the back of the room and carried it with me to the front. Then I laughed again as I looked at the dark bulk of the organ. Why hadn't it dawned on me before? The organ was electronic.

I crossed to the piano and opened it. This will have to do, I thought, setting the lantern beside the music rack and grabbing a hymnbook.

I turned to the first hymn. Number one, "The Morning Breaks." I laughed again. Perfect! I played it through a couple of times, hearing people in the chapel and gym begin to stir at the music's sound. I went on to number two. Thankfully, everyone seemed good-natured about being woken up, and before I got to number ten, the church hummed like a beehive.

At least there's one thing I can do.

CHAPTER SEVEN

Saturday, May 26

AFTER BREAKFAST, EVERYONE WORKED TOGETHER to repack the trucks and quickly clean the building. Another Mormon thing, I suppose. We weren't about to leave the church dirty, even if we never got the chance to come back.

Everyone gathered in the parking lot, and President Green got out his handy battery-operated megaphone.

"Wonderful job, everyone. We've made it through our first night on the road, and I want to compliment each one of you. May we keep this spirit of kindness throughout our journey.

"The next part won't be easy. Now we leave our vehicles behind and start our modern-day trek. I want to assure you that no one will be left behind. Those who can't walk will have a place in the green truck over there." He motioned to a large flatbed to his left, which, unlike the rest, hadn't been packed with supplies. Was I imagining it, or did he look directly at me?

"To the rest, the great majority of us, remember that God will help us. We're not used to walking all day long, and at first, it'll be hard. But it will get easier. We have each other to encourage us. Reach deep inside yourselves for strength, patience, and kindness. It will take all we have of those. We have doctors and nurses among us. We have food. We have water. We will be watched over.

"Here is our route for today. We'll continue down I-82 toward Prosser. It's fifteen miles. We're hoping to do more than fifteen a day, but for our first day, perhaps it's enough. And there's a chapel in Prosser, so that's a big plus. We'll remain there for the Sabbath. The pioneers didn't travel on

Sunday, and neither will we. Enjoy it, because after that, we're planning to leave the freeway for a time and take some smaller roads. We'll have to camp out—no LDS churches. I-82 passes too close to Hanford, so we'll go another way."

Only a few—some extremely elderly people and some younger ones in wheelchairs—were helped into the green truck.

One of the high councilors offered a prayer, and then most of the trucks pulled out. Just like that, the swarm of people moved out onto the road, picking up food for lunch off tables set up at the parking lot exits.

Two trucks, including the green one, followed behind. I felt the questioning glances from my family, but I pretended not to notice.

I was not going to ride in the green truck. No way.

The group soon spread out, with some folks walking swiftly, even running. Others moved more slowly, talking with friends and herding children. Many older folks, their gray heads lifted bravely, set off in their sensible shoes and cardigans. I saw Ryan walking in a cluster of girls my age, one begging to carry his guitar. I rolled my eyes.

I stepped out onto the highway. The pioneers would have loved this, I thought, as I looked at the smooth black ribbon of asphalt rolling across the hills. And then I started walking.

Why should it be any big deal? I mean, I could walk. Yes, I had a limp. Yes, I used a cane. So? I admitted I wasn't used to walking long distances. But I guessed many in the group didn't walk much. I knew farm wives who put off going to the mailbox at the end of their lane until they were out with the car.

I watched my Chuck Taylors as they moved step by step down the white dotted line. People stretched out across the road in front and in back of me for a long ways.

"Hey, Lee." Zack appeared out of nowhere, matching his steps to mine. "Let me carry your backpack."

I looked up happily, because this was the first time Zack had said anything other than terse answers to questions. Maybe he was starting to feel better.

"Oh, I'm okay." I shifted the strap a little higher on my shoulder.

"Come on, let me have it."

"Look, Zack, I don't want special treatment. Thanks though."

"It's not special treatment. I've carried your backpack a thousand times before."

"I'm good. For now. Don't get too far away though."

Zack shrugged. "Where am I going to go?"

We walked on. There wasn't much to see, although the landscape was pleasant enough, with spring freshening the fields with a light green tinge. Farmhouses squatted in the distance, but we didn't see anyone for quite a while. Then I noticed a few folks standing in their fields or on their porches, watching us as we passed. How odd we must look! I certainly didn't see anyone running after us, begging to join the group.

I'd managed to stay in the middle of the pack for the first half of the day. When I looked behind me, I saw the group had spread way out, with patches of walkers here and there and only a few large clumps. The two trucks bringing up the rear were specks in the distance.

At noon, we sat down on the highway's shoulder and ate the bread and fruit we'd picked up as we were leaving the church parking lot. Eating didn't take nearly long enough—two minutes later I was finished and feeling guilty about sitting down. But my feet ached, and my backpack had rubbed sore spots into my shoulders. I dreaded picking it up again.

Prosser was a fifteen-minute drive from Sunnyside—not even enough to talk about. On foot, time emphasized the big emptiness of the West over and over again. I remembered hearing once about the population density in some parts of the world—with a ridiculously high number of people per square mile. Well, they certainly weren't in southeastern Washington.

"I guess we better get going again," I mumbled and began levering myself to my feet with my cane. Zack picked up my backpack.

"Hey, give me that," I said as I straightened.

The dratted boy only smiled and jogged a few steps ahead, out of my reach. I shook my fist. "I'll get you, Zack Allman," I yelled, but I was too tired to argue.

I looked behind me. Mom stood but hadn't started walking. Ethan and Jarron still sprawled in their places on the weed-covered shoulder.

I gave the boys *the look*, and groaning in unison, they hauled themselves to their feet.

The unspoken thought we shared was, "If Cripple Girl can do it, you certainly ought to be able to." But I'd never say that out loud, and neither would they.

We set off again. A gentle hill sloped before us, practically unnoticeable in a car. I groaned inwardly. I felt every slight incline in the road.

We approached two guys sitting on the shoulder that I immediately recognized as missionaries. They still wore white shirts, although they had their sleeves rolled and ties pulled loose. Even if they hadn't had the telltale nametags and short hair, it was obvious who they were. That missionary spirit, I guess.

When we drew even with them, they stood up. "Can we walk with you folks awhile?" one of them asked.

"Sure," I replied.

"I'm Elder Shaw, and this is Elder Robertson," the taller one with brown curls said.

"I'm Amélie. This is my mom, Tina; my brothers, Ethan and Jarron; and this is Zack."

"I bet you never dreamed of doing this when you imagined your mission," Mom said.

They laughed. "I sure never did," Elder Shaw said. "This situation isn't exactly covered in the little white handbook either. In emergencies, we're supposed to go to the mission home. But since that's in Kennewick and super close to the Hanford site, I guess you're stuck with us."

"So you guys are missionaries?" Zack said, darting a glance my way.

"Yeah, watch out for them," I said with a smile. "They're the big bad baptizers I warned you about."

"I will." Zack grinned at the two young men. "So . . . the Elder thing—that must be a title—although you don't look exactly elderly. Are you supposed to keep your first names secret?"

Elder Shaw laughed. "No, no secret. My name's Josh."

Elder Robertson raised a hand. "I'm Ammon."

"Whoa, cool," Jarron said. "Like Ammon in the Book of Mormon? Ammon, man of arms." Jarron struck a bodybuilder stance. We all laughed, except Zack who raised one eyebrow.

"How is it—having a different name?" I asked, thinking of my own.

Elder Robertson shrugged. "I dunno. It's not that weird in Utah, where I'm from. It's cool."

We walked on companionably, my brothers peppering the missionaries with questions. Perhaps an hour passed. I was glad for the diversion.

I noticed two men had ridden by a few times, double horseback, going from one end of the group to the other and back again, passing us maybe once an hour. Now they reined in beside us. I was surprised when one of the men addressed me directly.

"Hello—I'm Brother Wilson from Yakima Second Ward," the man in front said. "Brother Cope and I are doctors, and we're just checking on the group. Making rounds, I guess you could call it." He laughed. "Are you doing okay?"

"Y-yes," I stammered. "I'm fine."

Brother Wilson nodded. "Great. Just let us know if—you know—it gets tough." I saw his eyes flick behind us, and I turned to see the green truck, much closer than it had been. I wasn't the last person, but we'd definitely dropped back in the group. I noticed there were quite a few more people riding than had been in the morning. Some lay with their heads in others' laps. Others sat upright but looked pretty haggard.

I could relate. My feet felt like they were about to break off, especially my right foot—the good one. My way of hobbling kept most of my weight on that foot. I'd step out with my right, then my left would touch ground briefly. Then it was back to the right. My whole body hurt from the sheer amount of walking.

"How much farther to Prosser? Do you know?" Mom asked.

I could have kissed her on the spot. I'd desperately wanted to ask that question but couldn't bring myself to say the words and sound like I was on my last leg or something.

"Not far now. Three miles or so. You'll be able to see it when we top that rise." Dr. Wilson motioned to a slope in the road.

Ethan and Jarron groaned good-naturedly, but I saw their eyes light up at the idea of closing in on our goal.

I forced myself to think only about making it to Prosser. At least tomorrow was Sunday. If I allowed a thought of getting up and walking a stretch just like this one tomorrow, I'd probably start crying.

One day, one step at a time.

Father in Heaven, bless me to be strong. Help me make it to Prosser. And, Father, do make it so President Green is right about it getting easier as we go, I prayed silently. *And bless Zack.*

Zack withdrew into himself again, not speaking a word once the missionaries left us. He still carried my backpack, and from the look of grim determination on his face, I wondered if he thought of it as a penance.

Not carrying my own pack made me feel like I was cheating somehow, but there wasn't a thing I could do about it. Zack walked near me, but it seemed the only reason was so he could wordlessly offer me water from the pack now and then.

At last we found ourselves walking through the quiet streets of Prosser—a town twice as big as Zillah. But two times nothing is still nothing.

I dragged myself into the church parking lot and threw myself onto the grass in front of the building. For most of the day, I'd been concerned about looking like a slacker, or worse—an object to be pitied and catered to. I was so over that. I didn't care what anyone thought as I flopped onto my back.

"You did it, Lee-Lee," Zack whispered, sitting down beside me. The look of tender concern on his face made my breath catch. He reached over and stroked my hair back where it fell across my face. I couldn't speak. All I could do was smile at him, and it broke my heart when he didn't smile back.

Thankfully, the routine of feeding and settling everyone went easier this time. The Prosser Ward building was pretty much just like Sunnyside—chapel and gym with classrooms, offices, and kitchen around three sides. It wasn't too cold, so several people opted to roll out their blankets on the grass outside.

I felt guilty, but I didn't move from my spot on the grass. Didn't help, didn't do anything. I must have dozed off, because some time later, I awoke to a nudge on my arm. I opened my eyes and saw a pair of boots standing near my head in the gathering twilight.

The boots connected to Ryan Cook's legs. "Hey, baby," he said, sitting beside me. "I brought you some supper. You gotta eat, you know." He set a dish of stew down in front of me.

"Huh?" I mumbled, sitting up and blinking the sleepy fog from my mind. Finally, his words plus the delicious aroma from the bowl added together to something that made sense. I held the bowl up and inhaled a tempting whiff of beef and potatoes. Food. I should eat. "Thanks."

"Long walk, eh?"

"Yeah," I managed to say between bites. I realized I was ravenous. I hoped I didn't look too piggish, shoveling the stew down like I was afraid it would get up and run away.

Why should I care how I looked to Ryan? I got angry at myself for even thinking that.

Truth was, it was hard not to care. He was Ryan Cook, with his cute, lopsided smile and his celebrity cachet, sitting on the grass talking to me. Only me. And he didn't act like he wished he could excuse himself and go somewhere else. He leaned back on his elbows and grinned. I caught myself grinning back. I also noticed those girls who'd been walking with him earlier eyeing me with envy.

I couldn't think of a single time I'd been envied before meeting Ryan, and I had to admit I liked the little twist of satisfaction I felt.

Now I was really mad at myself. Liking Ryan because he was famous was everything I hated. Fake. Shallow. At first I told myself the reason I liked him wasn't because he was famous, but because he was . . . he was . . .

Then I told myself to stop being ridiculous because I didn't like him, not like that. Hadn't I just been sighing over Zack? Good grief!

And what about Zack? My poor, wounded friend. How I wanted to make everything all better. Like it used to be. When we both had dads and one thing was crystal clear—we were best friends. These other feelings, whatever they were, scared me. What if it messed up things between us? I couldn't bear that. And always, nagging at the back of my mind, the thing I'd been taught over and over in Young Women and seminary: *date members of our faith.*

My mind still churned with those thoughts even after the group settled down to sleep. I understood the reasoning behind the dating members thing. I understood the thing about people marrying who they date, and I wanted a temple marriage. Someday. But I wasn't even remotely thinking about guys as marriage possibilities right now. I was an eighteen-year-old kid, for crying out loud.

Ridiculous. The whole thing was completely ridiculous. So what was my last stupid thought before drifting off to sleep? *Ryan's cute. And he's a Mormon.*

* * *

When I awoke, my body felt like frozen stone. I hurt everywhere but especially my feet, knees, and hips. I stifled a groan and stretched, trying to work some life back into my muscles. I forced myself to go down to the kitchen, where the women were making huge kettles of oatmeal, so I could offer my help.

I ladled out the pasty stuff as sleepy people shuffled by the kitchen serving window, laughing over a few good-natured jokes about how today everyone would be on time to church since we slept there.

Can't say we looked our Sunday best, though, as we settled into the chapel at ten a.m. Most people hadn't brought Sunday clothes—who could, when you could bring only one backpack? We did look odd, sitting there in our Levi's and unwashed hair, but being lined up in the chapel (and gym) and looking up at the familiar faces of the stake presidency on the stand lent an air of normalcy to the craziest Sunday of my life.

President Green opened the meeting. "I hope everyone slept well. Thanks to the Prosser Ward for letting us invade their building. They're on their own journey with the Kennewick stake, and no, I have no idea what their arrangements might be."

We had an opening song, with me at the piano. Afterward, I went back to my seat, and President Green returned to the pulpit.

"Our most important task is to partake of the sacrament." He nodded to the white-draped table to his right, manned by scruffy-faced members of the high council. "Then I'll spend a few minutes. Don't worry—church won't be a three-hour block today."

Zack squirmed beside me after the prayer on the bread. "Is everyone going to walk up to the front for the communion?" he whispered. "Will everyone stare if I don't?"

"Nope, you're fine," I whispered back. "We stay put. See?" We watched the men begin passing the trays, and Zack's stiff shoulder at my side relaxed.

When the sacrament was finished, President Green stood again at the mute microphone and raised his voice. He spoke for a bit on being brave and cheerful, watching out for each other, being kind, etc. etc., sounding pretty much like he wanted us to behave like good Boy Scouts.

"Now, brothers and sisters, thank you for your faith and obedience. Thank you for utilizing the chains of command. The bishops have relayed your questions, and hopefully you've received answers in return. Let me address some of the common concerns.

"We have some limited communication via ham radio. We can be grateful we live in the West in a sparsely populated area. Conditions in the large cities are pretty miserable. Certain areas are completely lawless, and the government struggles to cope with that, while at the same time it's trying to regroup, since DC was hard hit. May God bless them and the poor folks who live in those areas.

"Some have asked when it might be safe to return to our homes. I'm sorry to say that I still don't know that answer. It may be awhile before we know the extent of the radiation leakage from Hanford. Some ask why we have to go all the way to Utah—why not just go far enough to be out of range of the Hanford leak? That answer is simple. We are just too many. Utah is the only place with the supplies to sustain a group as large as ours. So Utah it is. That is the place for us, just like for the pioneers."

After the meeting, everyone enjoyed doing mostly nothing. There were meals to prepare and clean up, but we tried to rest and brace ourselves for a week of walking.

CHAPTER EIGHT

Monday, May 28

BISHOP TAYLOR PATTED MY SHOULDER the next morning. He wanted some wake-up music again, so I stumbled to the piano in the chapel as I had before. Luckily, some things came automatically for me, like playing hymns or finding the chapel in a Mormon church. I could do either one half asleep.

I raked my sleep-matted hair back from my face with one hand while the other riffled the pages of the hymnbook. At least I'm not a complete waste. I said a little prayer of thanks that President Green had the idea to ask me.

Gradually I began to forget myself as the soothing, familiar harmonies spilled out of the piano. I played as if I were playing prelude music, where I'd learned to disguise the end of one song and the beginning of the next so it all flowed together. "Redeemer of Israel" became "High on a Mountain Top" became "I Saw a Mighty Angel Fly." A prelude to a walk across the desert.

A few of us tried to wash our hair before we left the church. The water was running when we first arrived at the Prosser ward building, but it soon petered out. A couple of nice men brought a big water jug into the bathroom, and we took turns pouring water on each other's heads. We rubbed in a little shampoo and then attempted to rinse it out the best we could over the sink. The water froze my scalp, but having clean hair made me feel like a new girl. Such an ordinary thing felt like a true luxury.

We slowly left Prosser behind. I smiled to see I wasn't the only one feeling the effects of Saturday's long walk. The people near me seemed pretty good-natured about it though, mostly joking and laughing about their aches rather than complaining. Mom and the boys chatted with the missionaries again, and even Zack said good morning to me pleasantly enough.

The green truck brimmed with people—maybe forty now. Beside it, I noticed a wagon of sorts drawn by a team of four horses. Someone had rigged it from a light trailer and had stacked it with boxes and rolls of bedding. It hadn't been with the group before, so I assumed the leaders had acquired it in Prosser. I looked around, sizing up the group. Maybe it was bigger; I couldn't tell for sure. But it made sense that there would be people from this end of the stake who'd want to join us, and maybe this wagon held their contributions to the food and blanket stash.

Instead of getting back on the freeway, we turned onto Highway 221, the long snake of people funneling down onto the two-lane road as it curved off to the south. I couldn't help overhearing three men talking directly behind me.

"I guess President Green has his reasons for avoiding the main road," one said.

"Yeah, I heard he's concerned about roving gangs and whatnot," another replied.

"I'm sure that's part of it, but I also have to assume he's trying to give the Tri-Cities a wide berth. We still don't know for sure what happened at Hanford," the third voice said.

"The Tri-City stakes are surely evacuating too. Maybe they've arranged different routes for each stake so we don't clog up any one area with too many people," the first man said.

The men drew alongside us and then passed, still talking. I would have liked to hear the rest of their conversation, but I couldn't keep pace with them.

I scanned the sky. It was plain old ordinary blue with a few wisps of white clouds. It looked exactly like it always did. Looking northeast toward Hanford was no different. The thought that there might be something invisible and poisonous coming toward us through that innocent-looking blue sky was pretty creepy.

I wondered about EMPs and how they disrupt electronic equipment in the blink of an eye. What would have happened to airplanes flying up there in that endless blue when an EMP was set off? Would they drop like a stone? I shuddered.

Now and then we'd pass a car or truck, sometimes sitting on the shoulder and sometimes right in the middle of the lane. Did these vehicles suddenly stop functioning when an EMP invisibly burst through the air? Did they coast helplessly to a stop, stranding their occupants out here in the middle of nowhere? There was no way to know for sure, since there was never a sign of anyone around these abandoned vehicles. I pictured how confused these people must have been. No doubt they waited around for someone to drive by and offer help, but there was no one to come. Eventually, they'd have had to start walking this lonely stretch of road, unaware of the swarm of people who would follow their footsteps. When we came upon these vehicles, the group would flow around them without stopping, like water running past a rock jutting from a stream.

President Green wanted to keep us away from gangs and roving looters. That made sense, although there certainly wasn't any sign of crazy mobs out here. There was a whole lot of nothing, no matter which way I looked. Still, we carried large amounts of food with us—a valuable commodity right now. Perhaps the most important commodity. Men on horseback scouted ahead of the main group, and others rode beside the slow-moving supply trucks. I assumed they were armed. I shivered when I thought of what that might mean if we crossed paths with some truly desperate people. I thought of Zack and the gun he wore strapped under his jacket.

If Dad were here, he'd carry his rifle across his shoulders just to make sure we were safe.

Highway 221 connected Prosser to the little town of Patterson, but we only made it about halfway before the afternoon wore away. The supply trucks pulled off the road into an empty field. Perhaps it was someone's rangeland, but I saw nothing but sagebrush and tumbleweeds growing. Poor cows.

Maybe it looked like poor grazing, but at least I'd have to walk no farther. Here we would camp.

I was so tired and achy I couldn't think straight. All around me the Mormon Food Machine was cranking up, and I stood there, forcing back tears of humiliation. Okay, I hadn't ridden on the green truck, but I couldn't stand the thought of not pulling my weight in setting up camp. If one person thought, *Oh, it's fine if Amélie Hatch doesn't help with supper because—goodness!—she's got that leg,* I couldn't bear it. I knew I was being prideful, and no one said a word of reproach, but I knew. I'd been weighed and measured, and I'd come up short.

Mom, Zack, and the boys would have to take up the slack. The guys started unloading the supply trucks while the tail end of the group trickled into the campsite. Mom jumped in with the other women. I found a place to the side where I'd at least be out of the way.

A few minutes after the green truck pulled in with the last of the people, I saw a group coming toward us from the south. When they got nearer, I could see a couple of our scouts on horseback, and between them walked a group of nine Hispanic men.

They walked right by my resting spot as they came into camp. The men were filthy, with mud caking their jeans and smears of dirt on their arms and faces. One of them turned his large brown eyes on me as he passed, staring at me through greasy black curls that hung down his face. I cringed and looked down, ashamed of my fear.

"We need a Spanish speaker," one of the scouts called. "Where's those missionaries? They're Spanish-speaking elders, aren't they?"

Someone fetched the missionaries, and sure enough, they must have been Spanish-speaking elders, because they were soon chattering away with the nine men. I knew only a smattering of high school Spanish, but I did hear a few words I recognized.

"*Estamos Mormones*," one of the Hispanic men said, motioning with his hands to the others. "We're Mormon," he was saying.

Yeah, uh-huh. Maybe. And maybe we had food so they'd suddenly seen the light. I could imagine all sorts of people pretending to be Mormon in order to have a share of our food stash.

It's not like it was impossible that they were Mormon. There were two Spanish branches in the Yakima Stake, so there were Hispanic members in the area. Some of them were in our group. But I estimated the chances that these nine were Catholic to be about 99.99 percent. The chances they were hungry were about the same.

Why did they make me nervous? I prided myself on being totally free of racial prejudice and had several friends at Zillah High who belonged to minorities. It wasn't their skin color that was putting me on edge.

I examined my feelings carefully. Was it because they weren't members of the stake? That they hadn't been with our fellowship since the beginning of the journey? Was it because they might be Catholic? I laughed out loud at that thought. After all, Zack was Catholic. Maybe he was the most casual kind but still Catholic. Being Catholic had nothing to do with being dangerous.

I looked at the nine men, and a feeling stirred inside me. A bad feeling. How could I describe it? It was sort of like greedy fear. If we let those nine men travel with us, we'd have to share our food with them. Less for the rest of us. Less for my little brothers. Less for Zack and Mom. Less for me.

And then there was the niggling fear that we'd take them in, share our precious food with them, and then they'd turn on us somehow. It would be like picking up a rattlesnake and carrying it in your jacket.

The grasping selfishness grew inside me. I thought with shame that President Green would never have such feelings. Of course he would welcome the men.

Not everyone is hiding something, Amélie, I chided myself. Some people are exactly what they appear to be. Maybe they really are just scared, stranded men, just like they look.

I was the one hiding bitter, unworthy feelings.

I turned to see the captains, who had "circled the wagons," parking the vehicles in an arc around the rows and rows of bedrolls spread among the sagebrush. Several cook fires had been built in the hub of the circle. Black dutch ovens sat nestled in the coals. I wondered which one was ours—we'd dropped it off when we took our food storage to the bishop. I guessed it didn't matter anymore.

Bishop Taylor lumbered toward me. What could he want? There certainly wasn't a piano or organ out here.

"Sister Hatch, how are you getting along?" he puffed, shaking my hand.

"Oh, fine."

"Good, good. Listen, President Green wants you to give him a hand tonight. He's going to speak to the group—you know, a fireside-like thing, and he wants you to put together some music for everyone to sing. You know, opening song, closing song, that sort of thing."

"Me?" I squeaked.

"Sure. You're the music go-to girl, it seems."

"But, Bishop! Playing's one thing. That I can do. Singing and stuff's another. I don't sing."

Bishop Taylor patted my shoulder with a meaty hand. "Aw, you'll be fine. No one's asking you to sing a solo."

"But—"

"Now, Amélie, you might as well learn an important lesson right here and now about Church service. If you don't want to do something, delegate it. All you have to do is get it set up. It'll be directly after supper." He turned, leaving me sputtering.

Delegate it? As if I could do that. The only people I could make do stuff were my little brothers, and they certainly couldn't do this.

Then it hit me. A smile spread across my face as I scanned the crowd for a familiar curly head. Ryan!

There he stood, near the cook fires. I made a beeline for him, willing him to stay put till I could get over to him.

"Hey, Ryan," I said a bit breathlessly as I reached his side.

Ryan turned and smiled. "Hey, baby."

"Whatcha doin'?" I asked, trying for cool nonchalance, but I instantly regretted it. He was obviously doing exactly nothing.

"Oh, you know. Keeping the little kids from fooling with the fire. What're you doin'?"

"I actually need a favor. The stake people are having a big meeting with everyone tonight, and they want someone to lead us in a couple of songs. They've asked me to set it up. I'd be so thankful if you'd help."

Ryan's eyes flew wide. "Me? Play my guitar and sing? Hmmm . . ." He paused then grinned. "Thankful, eh? How thankful? What'll you give me?"

"Give you?"

"Yeah. What will you do for me in return?"

"Uh—"

"How about a kiss?"

I coughed, feeling a pink flush in my cheeks. I tried to laugh casually. "Oh, yeah, sure." Of course he was joking. I tried to assume the air of someone who banters about kissing all the time. "But, Ryan, it's gotta be, you know, like, hymns and stuff."

"What, I can't do 'Bluegrass Boys'?" Ryan grinned.

"Er—"

"It's okay. I can do hymns. I actually do know a few. Normally, I'd ask you to go through my agent, but for a kiss, I'll do it on my own."

"You will?" Relief washed over me, and I tried not to gush. "It's going to be right after supper." I turned, but Ryan caught my arm.

"What about my payment?"

"Huh? Oh! Now?" I looked around frantically. We stood smack in the middle of the entire stake. I imagined myself kissing Ryan Cook while everyone looked on. I must have turned a million shades of red.

And then the fleeting thought crossed my mind: *It would be your first kiss, Amélie. Is that how you want to remember it, forever and ever?* Like most girls, I'd spent time imagining what that first kiss would be like. I'd hoped it would be something special, something memorable.

Before the moment had a chance to get even more awkward, I forced a light, flippant laugh. "First you deliver the goods. Payment after."

To my relief, Ryan grinned and let me go.

I walked away, my thoughts a ridiculous jumble. One: relief because Ryan had agreed to do this music thing. Two: embarrassment because he'd said that thing about kissing me. Three: disgust at myself for thinking for one second he was serious, because he'd never want to kiss me. Four: fear that he was serious and that I'd make a fool of myself. Five: worry that I was getting a big, stupid crush on Ryan, and Zack would be the one hurt by it, even though he wasn't my boyfriend and wasn't even talking to me. Six: exhaustion from walking and apprehension about the nine scary men.

After a supper of sandwiches and Dutch-oven cobbler, the captains moved through the crowd, asking everyone to sit on their bedroll and get ready to hear some words from the stake president. Me, Mom, Zack, and the boys had just settled ourselves when the bishop approached me.

"Amélie, it's time. You better go on down front."

"Oh, I got Ryan Cook to do it. Just like you suggested." I smiled.

"That's fine, but you're the one who needs to follow through. Find him, and get it lined up."

"What's this?" Mom asked as I hauled myself to my feet.

"Just music they want for this meeting," I said. "Back in a sec."

I picked my way across the camp, looking for Ryan. Where was that boy? Finally I spied him, clear on the opposite side of the sea of blankets, pulling his guitar out of its case. I sighed and struck off in that direction.

"Hey, Ryan. It's time for you to go do your music thing. They want you down there by that little platform." I pointed toward the central area.

Ryan looked up from tuning his guitar. "Hang on. You're coming with me, right?"

"Uh, I was planning to go back and hang out with my family."

"No, you're the arm waver."

"Huh?"

"You know." Ryan drew a four-quarter-time pattern in the air. "I'm the accompanist and sing-along guy. I may not go to church that often, but I've been enough to know they always have an arm waver." He put a hand on my back and started to propel me toward the center area.

"Can't you do both?"

"No way, sister. I need both hands for Ashley." He patted his guitar.

I groaned. I hadn't gotten out of public humiliation after all. "Wait. You named your guitar Ashley?"

Ryan grinned. "Since roughly 15 percent of my target audience is named Ashley, it seemed like a good move."

I groaned again.

My heart fluttered with nervousness as we angled toward the center, where various captains and stake leaders were gathering. Then someone caught my arm.

I turned, and one of the nine strangers loomed before me—the same man who had stared at me when they'd walked into camp. I swallowed a squeak of fear.

His face was awash in agitation. He made talking motions with his fingers, pointed to my mouth, and then at the leaders. "*El Presidente.*" Then he gestured at the road winding to the south. "*Peligro.*"

I knew very little Spanish, but I'd heard that word plenty of times. *Danger.*

CHAPTER NINE

ALL I COULD DO WAS stare. Ryan tugged on my arm, and I stumbled forward. The man followed us.

We hesitated as we drew near the leaders, who were deep in conversation.

"There will be difficult choices ahead," one of the captains said. "Our food supply is just enough to take care of our stake, and it's tight. If we pick up many more stragglers, there won't be enough."

"The real question is, can we trust these people?" another man said. "I can't see turning them away, but how do we know if they might pose a danger to us? Our first responsibility is to our own."

"If it comes down to a choice between my kids having food or some stranger, I know what I'll pick," the first man said.

The Hispanic man burst from behind us and rushed up to President Green. Once again, he gestured to the southbound road. A stream of Spanish flowed from his mouth in a loud rush while he gestured wildly with his hands. "*Peligro.*"

Two of the captains rushed to the man's side and positioned themselves to protect President Green. One stepped in front of the Hispanic man, forcing him to take a step back.

President Green held up his hands. "Please, please. Do any of you speak Spanish? Can you tell me what he's saying?"

"I speak a little, but my mission was years ago," one captain said. "He is saying something about gangs, I believe. On the south highway."

"I've worried about this," President Green said, nodding thanks to the Hispanic man. "Soon we'll be to the mountain pass, and there's no practical way over except the highway."

"We've got to be careful no matter what," the first captain said. "It could be possible this man has his own reasons to divert us from the highway. Maybe he has people set up to ambush us when we turn from the main road. After all, we've got some pretty valuable cargo."

"That guy?" the second captain scoffed. "I seriously doubt it."

"How can we know? He's a stranger. People are desperate."

"We do need to be careful. Thank you, brethren, for your thoughts. There's much to think over." President Green looked up and seemed to notice me for the first time. "Let's start our meeting. Here's our music girl."

"Uh . . ." I'd wanted to tell him I couldn't be the chorister, but now I felt ridiculous bringing up my silly fears after listening to the much more pressing problems he had to deal with.

"Sister Hatch, what hymns have you selected? Ones to encourage us or ones to soothe our worries?"

I glanced at Ryan, who gave me a minuscule shrug. The entire group of men looked at me expectantly.

"Uh . . . ones we all know the words to," I stammered. "Since we don't have hymnbooks. Uh . . . how about 'Come, Come Ye Saints?'"

"Fine. And for the closing?"

"'Praise to the Man,'" Ryan piped up. "I've got that one goin' on."

President Green smiled. "And who is this?"

The thought that someone might not know who Ryan was stopped me for a moment. "This is Ryan Cook. He's going to be the accompanist."

"Great. And how about we swap them around? First Joseph Smith then Brigham Young, in a manner of speaking? Shall we begin?"

I nodded, my heart thudding as he stepped up on the little platform, which was not much more than a box.

How did this happen? I asked myself as I frantically tried to remember what meter "Praise to the Man" was written in. It wasn't supposed to be like this. I sought out my family in the crowd. When I found them, I saw Zack looking steadily at me. When our eyes met, he raised his fingers briefly in greeting. I took a deep breath and tried not to think about how many people were looking at me.

President Green raised his megaphone. "Brothers and sisters, thanks for your attention. We're going to have a little meeting now, and to add some normalcy to a crazy day, we're going to do it by the book. We'll have an opening song, 'Praise to the Man,' and then Brother Jacobsen will offer an opening prayer." He stepped off the platform and motioned for me to take his place.

Remember the power of music. Remember that music can take this crowd of tired, grumpy people and unite them. Remember that even though you'd rather crawl under a rock, this is a way to do your part.

I lifted both arms and smiled the fakest smile I'd ever given, letting my eyes go a little unfocused so I wouldn't see people staring at me. Beside me, Ryan played an introduction, and thankfully, someone thought to hold the megaphone close to his strings.

"Praise to the Man" always reminded me of "Scotland the Brave," and I let that thought go down deep, deep inside me. *Brave. Brave. Brave.*

I brought my arms down for the downbeat, and the crowd's voice swelled in my ears. One big glorious voice.

I nearly forgot to keep time when my eyes caught a glimpse of Ryan's fingers dancing across his guitar strings. The hymn was there, the four-part harmony intact so people could sing along, but he intertwined it with a clever picking pattern that made the song come alive. How did he do that?

I forgot about being nervous and let myself get caught up in the song.

Praise to his mem'ry, he died as a martyr;
Honored and blest be his ever great name!
Long shall his blood, which was shed by assassins,
Plead unto heav'n while the earth lauds his fame.

Standing there in the middle of the encampment, I could easily visualize the pioneers singing about their beloved Prophet Joseph. I felt their anger and frustration at being kicked out of their homes. No one had thrown us bodily out of our houses, but we'd been forced out all the same, even if it had been done by exploding a strange device high above us in the sky.

The song ended. Ryan tucked his guitar under one arm and held his other hand out to help me step down from the little platform. I took it, feeling the calluses on his fingertips against my palm. I smiled, not caring for the moment if the gesture was out of concern or merely to appear gallant to those looking on.

Why does he have to be so charming? I thought, angry at the way my cheeks flamed.

Brother Jacobsen prayed, and then President Green stepped up again, raising the megaphone. The familiar phrases of a Church talk fell on my ears like a comfortable blanket—thanking us for being there (I laughed to myself), thanking the Lord for His Spirit and asking that it might attend us. He talked about family, both our own and our larger stake family. He talked about testimony and faith and relying on the Lord for strength. He talked about being refined in the fires of hardship. The commonplace words almost didn't register as they simply created a feeling of peace. Then I realized he was saying something I'd never hear in the Zillah Ward chapel.

"There is danger on the road ahead. We have our scouts, we have our outriders, but as we cross the pass, we will be considerably more vulnerable. I continue to receive reports of trouble in the area. We may meet people who are in very desperate circumstances. It's not easy to know what to do. I've decided that if people ask us for help, we'll do what we can. There's a good chance this will make our short supplies even shorter, but I cannot turn people away who ask for help in good faith.

"However, if people attempt to take our stores by force, we must defend ourselves. I won't allow my people to be taken advantage of, and I won't stand by while mobs of grown men take food from our children."

A rumble of assent swept the crowd. Every eye fastened on President Green's face.

"I'll need more men. I'd like each captain of a hundred to select five more men, preferably those without young families, to form an additional guard. Without a doubt, this will be hazardous. No one should feel guilty about declining. If you have young children or aren't selected for this group, you can help by being vigilant within the main group.

"Now we'll sing 'Come, Come Ye Saints,' and while you sing, think of how our pioneer ancestors came together to form a fortress of strength. My dear brothers and sisters, this you can also do."

He stepped down and laid a hand on my shoulder. "Lead us, Sister Hatch," he said quietly.

By the time we were done singing, most of us were crying. Even Ryan had a funny look on his face.

"Thanks for helping. You were amazing," I said.

"No, you," he replied, his old grin returning. The tender, soft look from only a moment ago was gone.

"I'm going to catch up with my family." I pointed in their general direction.

"Sure. See ya, baby. Don't forget to pay up." He sauntered off toward his guitar case.

When I arrived back in our ward's area, several men were clustered around Bishop Taylor. Zack was right in the middle. I pushed close enough to hear their conversation.

"I have to be one of those five," Zack said. He folded his arms across his chest.

"Son, I appreciate the offer, but—"

"I know I'm not a member. But I *have* to be one of the five. I'm eighteen. I'm single. I have my own gun, and I know how to use it." His face looked stormy, like I'd never seen it.

Bishop Taylor gazed back at him and then at the surrounding men, seeming to size each one up, quickly ascertaining each man's family situation.

"The Hatches need looking after," Bishop Taylor said.

Zack darted a glance at me, and when our eyes met, it was as if our minds connected. I knew this was how Zack needed to take care of us.

"Let him do it," I called from my place at the side of the circle of men. "Please, Bishop. Let him feel a part of this."

For a moment, no one moved. Then Bishop Taylor nodded.

Zack looked steadily at me, his eyes alight. Then, with three long steps, he moved through the crowd to my side.

"Thank you, Lee-Lee." He put his hands on my arms. "I won't let you down."

"Zack, I'm so scared for you." I searched his face. The hurt look was still in his eyes, but behind that lay determination.

"Are you sure you guys will be okay?" he asked.

"You won't be far away. But you have to promise me, Zack. Promise you'll be careful."

"I promise."

Zack turned to Ethan and Jarron. "I'm depending on you two to look out for Lee," he said. "Don't let her get into trouble, okay? And watch over your mom?"

"Okay, Zack," Ethan said solemnly. Jarron nodded.

"Can you guys take turns carrying Lee's pack?"

"Sure."

I stared in amazement at my brothers. It was as if during the last sixty minutes, Zack and my brothers had mysteriously turned into men.

I was both proud and terrified for Zack. Maybe he knew how to shoot cans off a log, but what did he know about guarding our group against a mob of crazy people? An image of his bloodied, bullet-ridden body rose in my mind. I squeezed my eyes shut against the thought. *Have faith, Amélie,* I scolded myself. Faith. Courage.

Every fireside needs refreshments, and this one was no exception. The leaders surprised us. Along the way, they'd bartered with a farmer for fresh apricots from his orchard. He brought them out to us in cases stacked on an old trailer pulled by an even older truck. There was just one delicious apricot for each person. Mine tasted like heaven.

When it was time to sleep, we crawled into our sleeping bags. The ground was fairly flat but not as flat as the Primary room had been. There was a clump of weeds or something underneath me that prodded my back, but with a little wiggling, I managed to get semicomfortable. I pulled the bag right up under my nose, trying to minimize mosquito exposure.

Above me, sparkling stars and planets dusted the sky. Around me, crickets chirped and campfires crackled as they faded. Beside me, my brothers slept the untroubled sleep of tired young boys. I saw the glint of Mom's eyes as she lay on her back, staring into the heavens. Zack formed a silent huddled shape on her other side.

Once during the night, I heard a vehicle drive past on the freeway. One. Only one. Compared to the kind of traffic the road normally got, the fact that so few vehicles were untouched by the EMP was still shocking. Even in this relatively remote area, the freeway was normally fairly busy, with plenty of semitrucks hauling loads from place to place all over the West. I imagined the men guarding our camp had stopped the vehicle before it passed through our group to make sure it wasn't a threat.

It must have been a few hours later when I flopped over in my bag, my bones aching from lying on the hard ground. How long until dawn? My mind refused to drift off again. So much had changed in such a short time. Amélie Hatch: age eighteen. Address: seven sagebrush bushes left of I-84. This was the new normal.

The next morning when we left the encampment, the one hundred members of the new guard formed themselves around our group, walking and riding in clusters before, behind, and to our sides. More scouts were sent to join the others riding ahead, and I saw men walking several hundred yards to each side of us.

Even though I felt sick with fear for Zack, I felt a sense of relief. It seemed as if he had awakened from a walking coma. Now he talked and interacted with people around him instead of just going through the motions of walking, eating, sleeping. He seemed alive with purpose.

In spite of the excitement of the night before, the day passed without incident. We camped a few miles out of Patterson. This time, outside camping was much easier, having gone through the process before. Patterson didn't have an LDS church building, and we'd no doubt terrify the poor people if we went into town, since only a couple hundred people lived there.

Soon after we'd eaten, I saw a few men arriving back at camp, and I was glad to see Zack among them. He stopped to say a few words to Bishop Taylor and then hurried over to us.

"Zack!" I called as he approached. "How did it go? Have you eaten?"

"I have, thanks." He sat down on the ground beside us. "Pretty uneventful day, I suppose. We escorted the water truck to the river to refill it. They've got quite a setup—a generator, a pump, a nice filter system too. We did run into a couple of Oregon state cops out on one of the little side roads. They're here in camp with us now."

"Weird. What are they doing?" Mom said.

"They're talking with President Green right now. It's strange. The first thing they asked was if we'd seen a group of Hispanic guys."

"Are you kidding? Are they wanted or something?" I asked.

Zack shrugged. "Not exactly. But the cops are suspicious. They asked if the Hispanic guys were trying to get us to avoid the freeway, to take the back roads. You know, that's exactly what they've been trying to get us to do. The worry is that they are hoping to lure us into an ambush— that they'll get us off the beaten path somewhere and take all our supplies. I don't have to tell you how valuable they would be right now."

"Without supplies, we'd be . . ." My voice trailed off.

"Don't worry, Lee-Lee. We're taking care of stuff." He looked at Ethan and Jarron, at my pack lying at their feet. "How did it go today for you guys?" I saw the boys looking at Zack with new eyes. No doubt they wished they could be off protecting the group, scouting the area, packing a gun.

"Fine," they both chimed.

"But, Zack—" I laid a hand on his arm and let my voice fall soft. "How is it with *you*? I've been so worried. You seem a bit better now, but you hardly said a word to anyone for days."

"I'm okay," Zack said, his voice gruff.

"It's okay to miss your dad," I said. "I miss mine too. I know it's not the same with me, but it's still hard."

"I'm okay," Zack repeated.

I decided to change the subject because I didn't want to press him too hard. "So do you know if we'll follow the freeway or go on the back roads?"

"We'll find out soon enough. We'll have to commit one way or the other tomorrow. But I'm pretty sure we'll go on the freeway. I can't even guess how many days it would add to take another route. We don't have enough supplies to do that."

Later that evening President Green made an announcement to that effect, and the next day we found ourselves walking on the freeway. Thankfully, we'd be in Pendleton in three days, where there was a church we could stay in. Camping wasn't that bad, but having a real bathroom would be great. Perhaps there'd be showers too, and I didn't even care that the water would be cold.

After the brief respite of the chapel, though, we would begin the real test. Pendleton was the gateway to the Blue Mountains. When I thought ahead to what was to come, I got a flurry of fear in my gut. The freeway would enter a series of switchbacks, carrying us over the pass. We'd have days of climbing uphill. How would I manage? So far, the road had been pretty flat, but I'd still barely been able to drag myself into camp.

Don't think about those mountains, Amélie, I told myself. *One step at a time.* At least the road into Pendleton was still fairly flat.

The day wore on in a blur of plodding feet. Mom kept us smiling by singing Carole King and James Taylor songs in her thin, wavery voice. I ignored the sore place on my right palm where my cane dug in. I tried not to freak out that we were falling farther and farther back in the pack. The supply vehicles—and the green truck—practically licked at my heels.

Sometime in the afternoon, Zack jogged in from his assignment to the right side of the road to walk with us for a while.

"The Hispanic guys left our group," Zack said.

My mouth dropped open. "Are you serious?"

"Yeah. I guess they tried one more time to talk the leaders out of going this way. That Ammon missionary guy translated for them. When the leaders decided to go for the freeway, they left."

"Huh. What do you think about them? Do you think they really were going to try something?"

"Who knows. Those cops seemed to think so."

"Are the cops still with us?"

"Yeah, I believe so."

"Well, I suppose it's nice that if something weird does happen, we've got a couple more guys with a little experience to help out."

Zack smiled and, waving to us, loped off to the right, scaled the small fence that lined the freeway, and took his place on our right flank.

"Bye, Zack," I called. How long since I'd seen him smile? I hoped the old Zack was coming back, little by little.

In my heart, I knew Zack could never be the same boy he had been—before he saw his dad murdered right in front of him. Before he had to bury him, alone, without help.

"Dear Father in Heaven, bless Zack," I whispered under my breath while I watched his form shrink into a dark splotch against the hills.

The next morning, I woke up, blinking sleepy-eyed at the deep purple horizon. I groaned. Why had I awakened? It wasn't quite dawn, and I felt desperate for more sleep. I shifted to a less sore spot.

A cold drop hit my cheek. Rain! So that's why I'd woken up. Raindrops pattered on my sleeping bag, making little snapping sounds as they hit the nylon cover. A few more fell on my head, and I grabbed my damp pillow and dove under the cover of my bag.

I heard folks around me stirring as the rain roused them. Why did it have to rain now? In this part of the country, we often went weeks, sometimes months, without a bit of rainy weather. There were tents in the supply trucks, but most people didn't bother with them. I certainly hadn't. When we'd arrived in camp, I'd been too exhausted to think, much less set up a tent.

I peeped over the edge of my bag. It was raining in earnest now. Ew! The ground around me was rapidly turning to a mud puddle. I started to bolt from the sleeping bag for cover, but the ridiculousness of that hit me fast. Cover? What cover?

Some stake brethren had managed to put up an awning over the cooking area, but by the time it was fully light, everyone was drenched. Jarron, Ethan, and I hunched over bowls of oatmeal, trying to swallow it before too much rain fell in, water trickling down our necks. I watched the men and older boys breaking camp and loading the trucks with wet bedding and supplies. I felt sorry that they had to work in the rain and I was unable to help. We set off walking, miserable, cold, bedraggled, our shoes squelching with each step. The only good thing about getting started with the day's walking was that the freeway wasn't a muddy, gloppy mess like the campsite.

Not so much of an adventure now, I thought, stumbling past parents trying to chivy crying kids on their way. Mom shuffled wordlessly, head bowed, her peasant skirt sodden.

"Come on, Lee-Lee," Jarron said, tugging my hand. "It's just a little rain, right?" He looked at me hopefully, and I could see he was both trying to be brave and hoping I'd say something comforting.

"You're right." I forced a smile. "I mean, compared to a blizzard, like the pioneers, this is nothing. We're walking on asphalt, not across a river with ice floating in it. We have shoes. We have . . . stuff."

Jarron seemed cheered by my comment, and since Ethan mirrored Jarron's moods, they were good to go.

I turned my face to the gray, dripping sky. Now that I was thoroughly wet, what did it matter if rain pelted my face? I thought about the pioneers a bit more and, for the hundredth time, was glad I wasn't walking in petticoats.

Father in Heaven, how about holding back the rain? I prayed. *If this spot needs rain, how about later? In a few days, we'll be past this place. That would work better for me.*

The rain didn't stop. I sighed. We walked on.

It rained most of the day, and when we stopped to camp, I heard a guy say he was done and was going to turn around in the morning. President Green and the stake leaders talked to him, but apparently the visible reality of walking in the rain was worse to him than the invisible threat of radiation. They couldn't change his mind, and by the time we set off the next morning, six families and a couple other random people had turned back with him. What would happen to them? Would they get sick and die, or would they pick up their normal lives in their normal homes and normal beds? Or at least as normal as could be without electricity.

CHAPTER TEN

Friday, June 1

WE WERE LATE GETTING INTO Pendleton. The sunset lit the western skies with streaks of pink, purple, and orange. I'd always thought of the landscape around my home as bleak, but it sure put on a show at sunset. As we walked along in the fading light, I thought again that I was glad we didn't have to camp out tonight. That was so much easier to do when there was still daylight to see by.

All of a sudden, gunfire blared behind us. Mom screamed. Panic surged through me, and I felt my brothers pull in close to me. To protect me? Because they were afraid? I didn't know.

I whirled around and stared back up the dark road. The supply trucks had stopped. I could see dark forms running. There was shouting and more shots.

A clog of people ran toward the rear, brandishing weapons; others went forward in a crazed press of bodies. My heart beat wildly. I couldn't see Mom or the boys anymore. Had they followed the people fleeing forward? Or were they still right here somewhere? In the dark, I couldn't tell. Terror gripped me, and I tried to force myself to breathe.

Run! a voice yelled inside my head. But I couldn't run. I hobbled forward, praying I wouldn't fall while people all around me streamed ahead.

Leaving me behind.

I thought about the scripture that says something about, "Wo be unto them who are with child in those days," which I had been taught meant that in the last days, people would have to run for their lives and the poor pregnant moms wouldn't be able to keep up or would even be trampled in the rush. Well, I wasn't pregnant, but I thought they could have added, "And wo unto crippled girls," and not been far off the mark.

I stopped moving for fear I'd fall. I screamed, my voice lost in the tumult.

Some sort of scratchy cloth dropped over my head. Burlap. I couldn't see. Before I could pull it away, rough hands grabbed both my arms. My hands were pinned behind my back and quickly wrapped together with tape. My cane dropped from my useless fingers.

I screamed my throat raw. While I gasped for breath, choking from the dusty bag, I heard the sounds of men fighting very near me.

"Got one!" a voice yelled. I felt myself lifted, and my body doubled over a broad shoulder. Blood raced to my head. My cheeks scratched across the burlap with each of my captor's steps.

I screamed. I yelled. I sobbed when I could no longer make any sound. The noise of commotion lessened, and I knew I was being carried away from the group. Where was he taking me?

Someone shouted my name. More gunfire, deafeningly close. The man carrying me broke into an awkward run. My ribs bounced painfully against his bony shoulder.

"Hold your fire! You'll hit her!" shouted a voice I recognized as someone from the stake.

"Let's go!" someone yelled. I was dumped on something made of corrugated metal, apparently the bed of a truck. Doors slammed, and the vehicle leapt forward. The motion made me slide across the metal until I hit a barrier, perhaps the tailgate.

Someone near my head swore. Gunfire shattered in my ears. It sounded like there must be several men in the truck bed with me, firing weapons. The truck swerved, and I slid helplessly across the truck bed again. Pinball.

"Father . . . Father . . . Father in . . ." I tried to pray. I tried to breathe. It felt like my heart would beat its way right out of my chest.

The truck hurtled on for several minutes. Then it slowed to a stop, and I heard the clank of chains. Something scraped and creaked. A gate? The truck moved forward again a bit and then stopped. Many more voices surrounded me now, congratulating each other on their conquest.

Me. The hostage.

The same arms picked me up in a fireman's carry. Excited voices filled my ears, mostly bragging about how easy it had been to take me and how much of that great Mormon loot they would trade me for.

So they wanted our food. Of course.

The sound of my captor's footsteps changed, and I sensed we were now indoors. We seemed to move through a large echoing space and then perhaps a hallway. Finally the man stopped, and a door opened. He put me down and pulled the rough burlap off my head then cut the tape on my hands.

Four plain cinder-block walls closed in around me. The room was tiny, perhaps six feet square. A toilet sat in the corner. One chair sat alone in the middle. There was nothing else in the room but a small battery-powered lantern.

I looked up at my captor—one of the so-called cops who had been traveling with us.

He grinned. "Welcome to the Pendleton Pen. Make yourself at home." He stepped out, pulling the door shut after him.

I gulped at the panic rising in my throat. The prison! I'd seen the sign dozens of times alongside the freeway into Pendleton throughout my childhood. *Oregon Dept. of Corrections.* The inmates must have taken control of the place—probably when the power had gone out. I wondered if they'd killed the real cops they'd taken those uniforms from.

I wrapped my arms around myself to stop the shuddering. What would happen to me? My imagination turned into my enemy. I feebly tried to force my thoughts away from nightmare images of one helpless teenage girl captured by a gang of criminals.

Would our group negotiate with these people? Did I want them to? What if they demanded *all* of our supplies in exchange for my life?

They'll take everything and kill me anyway, I thought, sweeping an arm across the tears running down my cheeks.

And there's nothing I can do about it.

I sat down on the floor in the corner farthest from the toilet, trying not to think about what filth I might be sitting on. An hour passed, maybe more. There was no sound but my own sniffling. The lantern burned steadily, and I wondered how long it would be until the battery died and I'd be sitting in utter darkness.

I tried to pray again, but I couldn't focus my mind. I thought of Zack and his Catholic prayers. *Our Father who art in heaven, hallowed be thy name* . . . A rote prayer might actually come in handy at a time like this, I thought. Better than nothing.

The dead bolt snicked back. My heart leapt in my throat. Logically, I knew it was too soon to be thrown to the wolves—they'd still need me to bargain with—but my mind wasn't working logically at the moment.

The door opened, revealing the pretend cop. He had a gun tucked in his waistband, a bottle of water under an arm, and a piece of rough bread wrapped in a napkin in his hand. He set the bottle and bread on the chair.

"Bread and water seems a bit dramatic, but we don't have much food," he said, his face expressionless.

I glared at him despite my tears. "How could you? How could you do this?"

"How could I what? Do whatever it takes to stay alive?"

I thought of retorting, "How could you masquerade as a cop" or "How could you take advantage of our kindness" or "How could you take food from children," but I decided I'd rather not even speak to the creep. Besides, I was way too scared.

"Back later," he said. "For your sake, I hope the Mormons don't take too long to decide to cooperate. We're pretty desperate. Kind of you all though—bringing your stash right to us."

He stepped out, relocking the door. I looked at the stuff on the chair. Stories always described hostages refusing to eat, but I couldn't think why that would do any good in this situation. I also couldn't think of how it would benefit them to poison me. I stood up and sipped a little water from the bottle.

I paced raggedly, boredom interspersed with moments of terror. Was I minutes away from being gang-raped and killed? Would I be bought free only to watch my fellow stake members starve to death? I sternly told myself that just because I was weak and crippled, it wasn't my fault I'd been captured. If not me, it would've been someone else—I'd saved some poor grandma from being the one they snatched.

This was gonna take awhile. I sat back down. First, they'll have to deliver their demands to President Green. Then he'll have to decide what to do—maybe try to delay while they plan a rescue or maybe just load the stuff up and hand it right over . . .

Or maybe they'll decide they won't negotiate with kidnappers. Or that one girl's life isn't worth risking thousands going without food and supplies. Maybe they'll just leave me here.

I couldn't help hoping they'd think of a way to rescue me. But even that thought gave me the shudders. With both sides armed, it seemed impossible they could attempt a rescue without someone getting hurt. I imagined the scenario of President Green asking for volunteers to come in and break me out. I knew who'd be at the front of the line.

Zack.

Dear, loyal, brave, determined, foolish Zack.

I put my hands over my face, trying to repress another crying jag. For all I knew, he could already be dead or wounded after the firefight back at our camp. And my brothers . . . and Mom . . .

The lantern dimmed. After a few minutes, the cell was completely dark.

I couldn't judge time's passage as I sat there. I prayed like I never had before, just to keep my mind from unhinging. The completeness of the dark scared me almost as much as the thought of what crazy escaped prisoners might do to me.

Scooting into the corner, I leaned my head against the cinder-block wall and tried to unclench, relax. I hummed to myself. I played the piano on my knee. I tried to recite hymn lyrics. Maybe I dozed. Minutes, hours went by.

The clack of booted footsteps broke the silence, startling me even though the sound was faint. I strained to hear voices but could detect nothing but the steps approaching. My thoughts warred between fear of my captors and eagerness for light.

The door opened. Light from another lantern stabbed my eyes. It was the same man who'd brought me the food before.

"Oh, the lantern's already out?" He exchanged the dead one for the one in his hand. "Didn't mean to make you sit in the dark, but the fact is, we're low on batteries. We're pretty low on everything."

"How many of you are there?" I asked.

"Too many."

Our eyes locked as I considered the many ways I could interpret that. Too many of them for me to try to escape on my own. Too many of them for anyone to rescue me. Too many of them trying to survive in this place, making them desperate and dangerous. Too many of them for any one guy to control.

Which was it? Or was it all of the above?

He gave me a long, level look, and for a moment, I thought I detected regret on his face. Was there a chance he would help me?

Then his eyes grew hard again, and he abruptly turned and left, locking the door. I was alone. At least it wasn't pitch black anymore.

Time crept by.

The lantern dimmed a little, and I braced myself for impenetrable dark. But before the lantern had a chance to fade further, I heard voices outside the door. Not just the pretend cop this time. My heart raced. Several men. I told myself it was irrational for them to gang-rape me before they'd secured their trade. But my mind was like mush after hours of terror and nothingness. Reason left me.

The door swung open. Four men walked in, including Pretend Cop. The smell of their unwashed bodies filled the small space. I shrank against my cinder-block corner.

"We're going for a little walk," Pretend Cop said. "The Mormons have agreed to exchange you for the stuff, but they won't do it 'til they see you're okay. So we're gonna let them have a look-see."

I stared at him, trying to process his words. The stake had agreed to an exchange? But what would happen to us with no food or supplies?

"Well, come on, then. Get up." Pretend Cop nudged me with the toe of his boot.

I stiffly crawled to my feet. He retaped my hands then grasped one of my arms. Another man took the opposite arm. We shuffled into the hallway lit only by the flashlights they carried. As we passed, I could see it was a plain, empty corridor with several closed doors studding its sides. More holding cells, I supposed.

"Walk faster," Pretend Cop said.

"I can't, really."

"Why not?"

I felt my face burn. I hated explaining about my limp, and it seemed like I'd done it about a million times in my life. "I have a cripple leg."

Pretend Cop didn't say anything. But they pretty much dragged me along after that.

We rounded a few corners, picking up more men in our wake. The hallway opened into a foyer, with a guard desk in front of heavy double doors which were propped open. A few steps more, and they pulled another set of doors open.

Sunlight stabbed my eyes. Pretend Cop thrust me forward across the threshold, keeping a firm grip on my arm but stepping behind me. I realized he was using my body as a shield.

The other men drew guns. One of the guns pressed against my cheek, its hard steel firm and cold on my trembling face. The other men leveled their guns at a group of men standing at the end of a walkway leading up to the building. Blinking my eyes rapidly, I recognized men from the stake, including Bishop Taylor.

And there to the side, Zack.

"Here she is. You can see she's unharmed," Pretend Cop shouted. "Now do as you promised. Drive your supply trucks to that area." He pointed to a parking lot. "Then back off. We'll check the trucks out, and if everything's there, we'll release the girl."

One of our men waved his arm, signaling the supply trucks waiting down on the road. Slowly, they lumbered forward, crunching across the graveled parking lot. One, two, three, four . . . as far as I could tell, they brought up *all* of the supply trucks.

"No!" I shouted. "You can't give them all our food!"

"No comments from you," Pretend Cop said gruffly.

"Lee, are you okay?" Zack called out.

"Don't do it!"

Pretend Cop took the roll of duct tape out of his jacket pocket, tore off another strip, and put it over my mouth. Zack moved as if to lunge forward, but Bishop Taylor put out a restraining arm.

Dear God, don't let Zack do anything stupid, I prayed.

I couldn't believe they were going along with those insane demands. What were the stake leaders thinking? The journey to Utah had barely begun. We'd never make it without the supplies. It wasn't like we'd be able to get more along the way. If there was food available around here, these prisoners would have found it already. Tears squeezed from my eyes.

The drivers climbed out and backed away from the trucks, joining the group of our men. I shook my head in dismay.

Please let this be a bad dream. Please let me wake up, I prayed. The whole stake was going to suffer to buy my way free.

If they even keep their part of the bargain and let me go—they're a bunch of prisoners! Who knew what they were in prison for, but did it really matter? They all had to be killers by now. Their guards were all gone, and something told me they didn't just walk away.

"We're gonna check the trucks out now," Pretend Cop shouted. "I hope for your sake there's nothing funny about it, seeing as how there's still a gun on the girl's head. One sign that you're trying something, and it's over."

A group of men, armed with rifles, cautiously approached the trucks and raised the roller door of the first one. Two men climbed inside while the others remained on guard, weapons at the ready.

"This one looks good," one of the men called after a few minutes. They searched each truck in turn, and I felt my heart sink as it became clear there was no trick, no fancy bait and switch. No men with guns poured out from secret hiding places. The trucks were full of food and supplies. Nothing else.

I glued my eyes to Zack's face. Would they really let me go? I imagined them saying the word and Pretend Cop shoving me off toward our group. I pictured stumbling across the walkway, and then maybe Zack would meet me partway, and he'd catch me up in his arms . . . and he'd cut my hands free . . . and then . . .

The men returned from checking out the trucks, and the group conversed quietly. I couldn't understand much, although they stood fairly close.

Pretend Cop raised a hand. "Okay, it looks pretty good. So far. Problem is, we're gonna need more. We're gonna need whatever livestock you guys have got. Horses, cattle, all of it. So we'll just take the girl back in for a bit, and you all round up the animals and bring them on up here. Then she can go."

Our men shouted in outrage. "No way!" Zack yelled. "She's going free *now*." He stepped forward, and this time no one pulled him back.

CHAPTER ELEVEN

Saturday, June 2

"WE'VE GOT TO SHOW THE Mormons we're serious," the prisoner holding the gun on me said. He took the gun away from my face and pointed it at Brother Smith, who'd stepped up with Zack.

He pulled the trigger. A deafening crack exploded in my ears. Zack leaped sideways in front of Brother Smith and then staggered back, falling across the other man's arms. Red blossomed on his shirt.

I screamed behind the piece of duct tape on my mouth. *Zack! No!*

Our men started shooting. Guns came from their pockets, from behind their backs, from thin air, it seemed. I guess they'd hit their breaking point. Men around me fell like stones.

"Get down, Amélie!" someone yelled above the cacophony. I flung myself to the ground, shock spreading through my body.

Zack!

I rolled to my side, behind the fallen body of a prisoner, wishing I could wrap my arms around my head, but they were still taped together behind my back. Part of me wanted to peer around the body to see how many of our men were still standing, still shooting. And to look for Zack. To see if . . . No, I couldn't bear to even think about whether or not he was dead.

The crack of gunfire slowed. Strong arms grabbed me, and I felt myself lifted. This time, instead of riding a bony shoulder, I was enveloped in the big meaty arms of Bishop Taylor.

"We're getting out of here," he said. I couldn't respond. Even if there'd been no duct tape on my mouth, I doubt I could have unclenched my teeth enough to talk. He strode down the walkway and across the parking lot to one of the supply trucks. The driver's side door stood ajar, and he thrust me onto the seat. He climbed in after me while I hitched myself over to make room. He slammed the truck into gear, and we wrenched out of the parking lot, spraying gravel right and left.

I could see at least one other truck behind us. Did that mean our men had routed the prisoners? Or did some brethren lie on the pavement, never to walk the highway again?

And the question I couldn't bear to ask but couldn't live another minute without knowing the answer: what about Zack?

Bishop Taylor muscled the truck onto the highway, driving the few miles back to our camp.

When we pulled to a stop at the edge of camp, I could see worried people hurrying toward the truck. Bishop Taylor turned to me as soon as he removed the keys from the ignition. "Sorry there wasn't time to get this stuff off you 'til now," Bishop Taylor said gruffly, easing the duct tape off my face. "I had to be sure we could get clear."

"It's okay." I twisted so he could use his pocketknife to cut the tape on my hands. I rubbed little balls of glue off my face and wrists. "Bishop, what happened? I couldn't see. Is anyone . . ."

"Let's find out."

The passenger door opened. There stood Dr. Wilson. Right behind him were the worried faces of Mom and my brothers. Relief washed through me. They were okay.

"Thank goodness," Dr. Wilson said, holding out a hand. "Let me help you over to the medical tent."

"I'm fine." I took his hand to climb out.

"Oh, Amélie," Mom said. We hugged each other hard, all four of us.

"Let's check you out," the doctor insisted.

"Really, I'm fine," I started to protest, but the thought came to me that if Zack was still alive, the medical tent would be where they'd take him. That was where I wanted to be. I put my hand on the doctor's arm and let him lead me away, Mom and the boys right behind.

People crowded the medical tent, and I craned my head this way and that, hoping to see Zack's familiar form.

They wouldn't bring him here if he were . . . if he were dead. I felt a little stab in my chest as I glimpsed the doctors' cots between the shifting bodies. There were four cots, one occupied. Not Zack. Panic clamped down. I forced myself to breathe in, out.

"Make way!" a man's voice shouted. "Clear the tent! Everyone out!" Two men carrying someone sidled in, the people parting before them. I couldn't see the injured person's face, but I recognized Zack's boots dangling over the man's arms.

"Zack!" I cried. Someone herded people out of the tent. Would they make me leave too? I followed Dr. Wilson as he rushed forward to the cots.

I found myself looking down at Zack's still face. All three of the camp doctors knelt around him, cutting away his bloody shirt. Zack's face was pasty, and his eyes were closed. He looked like a corpse.

The doctors spoke to each other in anxious, hurried voices, using medical terminology I couldn't understand. I stared at the angry wound in Zack's gut as the doctors' hands fluttered over it. Blood was everywhere. I sat down hard on the cot beside them, my head buzzing.

"He's not going to make it," I heard a voice say, fuzzy and distorted as if in a dream. "Maybe if I was in my operating room . . ."

"He's gaining consciousness," another said. "Is the anesthetic ready?"

"Amélie, come with me," a voice spun around my head. "Let's give the doctors room." Hands lifted me to my feet.

President Green ducked through the tent opening. He laid a hand on my shoulder. "Glad you're safe, sister." He turned to the doctors.

"President, we're getting ready to operate," one said. He opened his mouth to say more but glanced at Zack, whose eyes fluttered weakly. He shook his head instead.

"Is there time for a priesthood blessing?" President Green asked.

"That would help more than anything we can do."

President Green moved to Zack's side and picked up his hand. "Hello, Brother Allman. These doctors are going to help you. First, though, I'd like to give you a blessing. Would that be all right with you?"

Zack looked back at President Green, his eyes full of pain and questions. "You know . . . I'm . . . Catholic?" he whispered.

"That's fine, son. Do you have faith that God can heal you?"

Zack hesitated. "Yes."

"That's all you need. Just lie there easy."

President Green and Dr. Wilson laid their hands on Zack's head. I held my breath, waiting for the certain words I longed to hear.

I knew very well sometimes those words weren't said. I knew from firsthand experience. After all, I'd had lots of blessings in my life from my father's humble hands.

He'd given me many wonderful blessings, including strength, perseverance, and faith. But he never felt prompted to take away my lameness. He apologized every time, even though I knew it wasn't his fault. Apparently God thought I still had something to learn.

President Green prayed that the Spirit would be present. He blessed the doctors that their hands would be skilled. And then I heard the words: "I bless you that you will be healed, both your body and your heart, according to your faithfulness." *That* feeling came over me—not the everyday, nice, comfortable feeling of God's presence but that rare, beautiful, intense feeling of the Spirit I'd only experienced a few times in my life. It felt like I'd burn up from the inside out, yet it felt wonderful. It filled me to bursting.

He said a few more things that I scarcely heard because I was crying, and then it was over. The men took their hands from Zack's head.

"What do I do now?" Zack asked.

"Now you exercise your faith."

The doctors put a mask over Zack's face, and someone led me out of the tent.

I realized it was Mom. I pressed my tear-soaked face into her blouse, and that's when I really let go. All the pent-up tears spilled out—tears for Zack, Dad, our home, our old comfortable life. Because I was scared and exhausted. Because I was too distraught to go on trying to be brave and strong.

* * *

The waiting was awful. Mom and I sat holding hands outside the medical tent until the sun went down. Meanwhile, I whispered my tale of being kidnapped, the cell, and the shooting. Thankfully, Mom just listened— no freak-outs this time. Lanterns shone from inside, projecting shadowy images on the tent wall. At last Dr. Wilson came out. Even though I'd braced myself for it, the sight of blood covering his clothes still shocked me.

"He's sleeping," Dr. Wilson said, his shoulders drooping tiredly. "We'll know more tomorrow. If he makes it through the night, that'll be a good sign."

Mom slipped away for a few minutes and came back with our sleeping bags. I smiled my thanks. We curled up in our bags as close to the medical tent as we could.

I lay on my back, looking up at the night sky arcing overhead. I was exhausted, but the uncertain fog of the past few hours seemed to recede as I stared into the velvety blackness smeared with stars. The thought crossed my mind that those light specks were actually giant, swirling balls of gas, and it made me feel even more insignificant than usual.

I thought about the blessing Zack had received. I knew God could heal him. But would He? Did God notice the little cares and concerns of one puny girl? I immediately felt guilty for thinking that and hurriedly shoved the thought away. What if my doubts jeopardized Zack's chances of being healed? I shivered with fear for Zack and at my own weakness.

I tried to pray but gave up when my prayer kept veering into a bargaining session, with the usual promises of transforming myself into a pillar of piety if only Zack would be allowed to live.

I'm sick and tired of feeling weak, scared, and alone, I thought. *I'm tired of pretending.*

I thought about Dad, and the fact that no one would tell me a thing about him got me all churned up inside again.

"Mom? Are you awake?"

"Yeah."

"Where the heck is Dad?" I didn't really expect an answer.

"At this precise moment, I have no idea."

As usual, me badgering her about Dad made her start crying. She sniffled and gulped loudly for a few moments. I sighed then reached over and took hold of her hand. I squeezed it reassuringly and talked softly to her of better times until she fell asleep.

* * *

The sound of footsteps approaching woke me. I sat up, rubbed my face with my palms, and clawed my fingers through my tangled hair.

"Good morning, Sister Hatch," President Green said. "I'm about to check on your friend. How was the night?"

"Quiet. No news is good news, I think," I replied. "No one's been in or out." I paused. "President, may I ask a question?"

"Sure."

"Why did you decide to give our supplies to those people? I mean, I'm grateful, but it doesn't seem logical to risk everyone's life for mine."

President Green smiled. "Your life is worth everything to us. But we did have a plan. Not the way it happened though!" He shook his head ruefully. "You see, we put several gallons of fresh milk that we'd bartered for in the supplies we delivered. We figured your captors would love to have some of that. Before we took the stuff up there, the doctors infected the milk with a flu virus that's been going around camp. We planned to wait a few days until enough of them came down with it. Then we'd go in and take our supplies back. It seemed like the perfect plan. They wouldn't get sick right away, so they wouldn't suspect anything. They'd give you back, we'd bide our time, and then we'd get our stuff back with a minimum risk." He shrugged. "Obviously, that's not the way it turned out."

The Hispanic guys. They'd tried to warn us. Would we ever have a chance to thank them?

My head filled with memories of that chaotic moment when the shooting started. The noise . . . bullets whizzing around . . . I realized I hadn't seen much of anything after Bishop Taylor had scooped me up. "President, I feel bad that I don't know this, but—did any of our men get hurt besides Zack?"

President Green looked down a moment then back into my eyes. "Yes, I'm afraid a couple of men did get hurt. But not in the way you're thinking. Physically, they are unhurt. But they ended up shooting—and killing—three of the prison men."

"Oh." A sick feeling spread over me. People had been killed. I knew the stake men involved would be forever changed. Even if I hadn't watched Zack go through the same experience, I knew using a gun against another human being couldn't be shrugged off. I told myself the prison men had shot first. I told myself the stake men were defending more than me—they were defending their families' right to survive. Maybe the thoughts made sense, but they didn't make it any easier.

He looked at me kindly. "A couple of the men said Zack stepped in front of Brother Smith when the guy shot at him. Is that the way you saw it?"

I nodded.

"Do you think he took that bullet on purpose?"

I could only stare back at him wordlessly.

"Why don't you come check on Zack with me?"

I scrambled out of my sleeping bag and swiped at the clothes I'd slept in. Mom stirred beside me but didn't fully awaken.

We stepped nearer the medical tent. I hesitated with my hand on the flap. What would I see? I bit my lip, trying to shore up my courage. It was possible Zack hadn't made it through the night and the doctors had decided to wait until morning to announce the bad news. I might duck through the tent flap and see a corpse.

It was also possible he was still clinging to life but by the thinnest thread. Maybe he was in a coma. Maybe he would never open his eyes again.

I felt President Green's reassuring hand on my shoulder. I drew in a deep breath and parted the flap.

Zack was sitting on the edge of the cot. When he saw me, he smiled. He was alive! He was more than just alive!

"Zack!" I wanted to throw my arms around him, shout, sing, pray, laugh, and at that moment, I think I even could have danced. I rushed toward him, ready to do all of it. But then I stopped short. There was a difference after all—his cheeks were wet with tears. And all at once, there were tubes, bandages, and doctors, like barriers between us.

All my pent-up fear and doubt released in big shaking sobs. I sat down beside him, carefully avoiding the trailing tubing, and picked up his rough farmer's hands, squeezing them between mine.

"Lee-Lee . . . I'm healed," Zack said, his voice hushed. "They said I was bleeding pretty bad inside, but after that special prayer, that blessing, I was all right. All this stuff"—he motioned to his middle and his IV-punctured arms—"is just so the doctors can make sure everything's okay." He looked at me, his eyes filled with wonder. "I should have died, Lee. The doctors said . . ." He broke off and looked at Dr. Wilson standing near him.

The doctor nodded. "Clearly a miracle," he managed to croak, his own emotion thick in his voice.

"I don't know what you did, but thank you," Zack said to President Green.

"It seems God has plans for you. He needs you."

Zack looked stunned at that. We sat quietly a moment, then he responded. "Maybe God just needs this caravan to keep moving. I'm ready to travel. There's no need to wait on my part."

"That's great, son. Truth be told, I'd like to leave this area as soon as possible. I don't like hanging around the prison, and we've got a long way to go. Today being Sunday, we'll stay put, but we'll aim to leave in the morning. Sacrament meeting is at two."

Sunday! I hadn't even realized what day it was.

I thought of the Blue Mountains looming just ahead. A week ago I'd been so apprehensive about trekking over them I could hardly sleep. But now, for the moment at least, I felt filled with strength. God was with us. We could cross those mountains.

President Green continued. "There's room for you to ride in one of the supply trucks to give yourself time to heal."

Zack winked at me. There'd be no green truck for either one of us.

* * *

Pendleton faded behind us. I was never so glad to leave a place. I hoped I'd never see the Pendleton Pen again.

Zack walked beside me, our faces turned toward the mountains. I'd lost my cane in all the commotion of the kidnapping, dropped it somewhere on the dark highway. Instead, I held Zack's arm lightly. Once upon a time, doing that would have made me crazy. Now, I was happy for the excuse to keep him near.

Was I falling in love with Zack? In a grown-up, woman-loves-man sort of way? I shivered when I remembered how piercing the pain had been when I thought he'd been killed. But that alone didn't mean love. A person could feel that way about losing a close friend, someone they'd been through so much with in such a short lifetime, couldn't they?

All I knew is I wanted to be with him, hear him talk, watch him move, feel his warm skin under my hand. In my mind, I prayed a running stream of thanks for his life.

The fact that he wasn't a member of the Church had made it convenient to let things be. To just stay friends. But after everything that had happened, I couldn't help hoping there was a chance the light would turn on for him. He'd get a testimony. He'd get baptized. And that would change everything, wouldn't it?

I ached to ask him if traveling with us all this time and then his miraculous healing had made him wonder if there was something to this Mormonism stuff after all. But I was terrified I'd say it wrong and mess everything up. I opened and shut my mouth about twenty times. In the end, it was Zack who broached the subject, oblivious to my falterings.

"Lee-Lee . . ." Zack's voice sounded hesitant.

"Yeah?"

"Does that sort of thing happen all the time to Mormons? People getting healed?"

I was tempted to say, *Oh sure! It's miracles all the time with us. Try it, you'll see!* Instead, I forced myself to take two breaths, send up a microscopic prayer, and think before responding.

"God answers everyone's prayers, Mormon or not. But yes, there are miracles now and then. Like yours."

"Have you ever been healed? Like that? With the hands-on?" His eyes flicked down at my lame leg, and he bit his bottom lip, as if wishing he could call the words back.

"Actually, I have. Lots of times."

"Really? The stake president goes around to people's houses and heals them?"

"My dad did it, mostly."

"Your dad? But he's a regular guy, isn't he?"

I laughed. "Yeah. But he has the priesthood, and any worthy man who has that can bless people. Most Mormon dads do . . . Like the time I got my first migraine. I'd never felt a headache so bad. It scared me. Dad gave me a blessing, and the headache went away. Right then."

I stole a sideways look. Zack looked shaken.

"But sometimes—" He broke off.

"Yeah, sometimes." I nodded. "Healings and stuff happen according to people's faith. But it has to be God's will." The words were underscored by the thump of my uneven steps.

"So it was God's will that I have this miracle happen to me," Zack said, his voice soft and full of wonder. "Why me?"

"That's what you've got to find out. Maybe God's got something special He needs you to do. Maybe He wanted to show you He's there. Maybe He's sending you a message."

"How am I going to find out?"

"Pray, mostly. And listen."

We fell silent, both lost in our thoughts. I wondered if Zack was used to praying, other than saying the rosary.

CHAPTER TWELVE

Tuesday, June 5

THE ROAD STARTED INCREASING ITS slope in earnest. I trudged along between Zack and Mom, with Ethan and Jarron on each side of us. I was determined not to get discouraged as more and more people flowed past us. I didn't notice Ryan.

It seemed everyone wanted to say something to the miracle kid. Everyone knew what had happened—how he'd been shot during my rescue and then healed. Maybe people thought he was the group's good luck charm and that to shake his hand or touch his shoulder would transfer some of that good luck to themselves. Zack was flustered by all the fuss, and I fretted that someone would say the wrong thing. What if a well-meaning person came up to Zack and demanded to know when his baptism would take place now that he'd been the recipient of such a gift?

That was the last thing I wanted. I didn't want Zack spooked by good-intentioned but overzealous members or to feel cornered or pressured. Things needed to develop naturally.

I wanted to keep walking rather than sit down to eat lunch, hoping to make up some of the distance since I'd fallen behind in the group. My brothers seemed antsy at my slow steps, but Zack seemed content to keep pace with me. I noticed him touch his middle now and then, where bandages still wrapped him beneath his clothes. I guessed that in spite of a miraculous healing, his body still worked to recover. We were quite a pair, limping along.

We reached an overlook I remembered driving past in a car many times before. Miles and miles of cropland spread out around the foothills we climbed, looking strangely peaceful and ordinary. At least a hundred people had stopped there for a break. I fought on.

In just one day, I saw the dry, flat landscape transform into steep, piney mountains. Evergreens crowded the roadsides. I tried to focus on their quiet beauty to take my attention away from my aching legs and straining lungs. At least we walked in the shade of the pines—a pleasant change. Sunlight dappled the asphalt in golden streaks.

"Lee-Lee, honestly, it's okay to stop for a few minutes," Zack said. I darted a look over my shoulder, seeing only a few stragglers between us and the green truck. "Or hey, you could ride piggyback for a little while. Might be fun."

I glared my response then nearly fell trying to speed up a little.

"What? Are you saying my rippling muscles aren't up to that? I take great offense. After all, you're pretty puny."

I couldn't help laughing. "No *way* am I riding piggyback."

We passed a road sign proclaiming we'd reached the summit of the Blue Mountains. "Deadman Pass, elevation 3,713 ft." I knew from previous car trips to Utah that there were plenty more hills left between here and Utah and a couple thousand feet of rise, but this was the steepest bit to do all at once. I let out a victory yell, and Zack pumped his fist.

One last half-hour push and we gratefully dragged ourselves into camp, already being assembled by the swifter-walking folks.

"'Emigrant Springs State Park,'" I read aloud from a sign. "That means bathrooms! I don't even care how wretched they might be."

We ate dinner as the sun set. Zack and I weren't the only ones who were tired after that ascent. The camp was pretty quiet, and many found their bedrolls before it was even dark.

I looked around for Zack and couldn't find him at first. At last I saw him sitting by himself at one of the fire pits, working on something long and slim in his hands. I sat next to him on the log that had been pulled up as a seat.

Zack looked up, startled. "Hey, don't look!" He shoved whatever was in his hands behind him. "Close your eyes. I'm almost done."

"What's this? A surprise?" I put my hands over my eyes.

There were a few scuffling, scraping sounds. "Just about . . . hang on . . . okay, there. Hold out your hands, but keep your eyes shut." He placed something long and cylindrical, about the thickness of a broom handle, in my hands.

"Okay, open."

In my hands was a length of wood that had been scraped and smoothed. "A cane! You made me a new cane."

"Do you like it?"

I glided my hands along the wood. "I love it. Thank you, Zack." I laid it across my knees and hugged him impulsively, like I might have done for anyone who'd been especially nice to me. Like a brother.

Zack hugged me back, his arms light across my shoulders. But all of a sudden, it didn't seem so brotherly, and we broke apart. I felt my cheeks heat, glad the darkness covered me.

"Zack, why'd you do it?"

"Well, I don't mind you hanging on my arm, but I thought you'd like a new cane. I know it's not nice like your store-bought one—"

"No, no. Why'd you throw yourself in front of that bullet? You don't know Brother Smith that well. You risked your life for him. Without a miracle, you would have died."

Zack stared into the fire for a long time. "Because I was a throw-away. Damaged goods."

"What?" I couldn't believe what I was hearing. *Damaged goods.* That was my secret name for myself. Hearing Zack describe himself that way sounded bizarre and wrong.

I refused to carry that thought on to the idea that if it was wrong for Zack to call himself damaged goods, it was wrong for me as well.

"I only had a moment to think, but it seemed like a good trade at the time. A screwed-up life in exchange for a guy with kids and stuff."

"What do you mean, screwed up?" I demanded.

"You know exactly what I mean. No family, nothing. Out in the middle of nowhere, living off the charity of a bunch of people I don't belong with."

I started to protest, and he raised his hands in defense. "I know, I know, you asked me to come, and I appreciate it. But even if I wasn't an outsider, there's still the other thing."

"What other thing?"

"Do I have to say it? I killed a man." The words spilled between his clenched teeth.

At first I thought maybe he meant he'd shot one of the prisoners, but I knew that couldn't be the case. Or that he blamed himself for the start of the gunfire. Then I knew he meant the guy he'd shot through the windshield of his dad's pickup.

"Zack, you can't torture yourself about that. It wasn't like you set out to kill a man."

"Well, what was it, then? It wasn't self-defense. They were already in the truck, driving away. I just freaked out. I aimed at his head, and I pulled the trigger. What do you call that?"

I swallowed. I honestly didn't know what to say.

It was one of the most awkward moments of my life. *What do you call that?* repeated in my mind. That act, whatever it was, couldn't possibly be called murder, deserving God's harshest condemnation. Could it?

Zack stared straight ahead into the fire, his face stony. Every second that ticked by while I struggled to reply felt like *stab, stab, stab.*

"Zack, I don't know the official word on this. But I do know God loves you. He knows your heart. He knows all the circumstances surrounding what happened, every one. No matter what we do, He still cares about you, me, everyone."

"How can you possibly know that for sure?" he whispered.

"He tells me in my heart." I placed my hand on my chest. "He'll tell you too."

"Maybe you'll have to ask Him for me. I don't seem to have the praying thing down. You, on the other hand . . . you and God, you're just like that." He held up two fingers and then crossed them.

"Look, Zack, if what you did was a sin, God will forgive you."

Zack's hands found mine. "What I need to know right now is if *you* will forgive me. I'm not like you, Lee-Lee. You're so—you're so—"

I'm so what? I thought. So self-righteous? So preachy? So helpless? So burdensome?

"You're so beautiful."

And then he kissed me.

It was a little awkward, my first kiss and all. But Zack let me try again, and the nearness of him made my heart thunder in my throat. He stroked my hair as if he thought it was nice and held my face between his hands as if he wanted to look at me, and for a moment, I could nearly believe I was beautiful.

CHAPTER THIRTEEN

Wednesday, June 6

IN THE MORNING WE WALKED silently together. My mind hummed with thoughts, mostly reliving the pleasant memory of the night before.

Those thoughts quickly went way out of control. If Zack thinks I'm beautiful, does that mean he loves me? If he loves me, does that mean he wants to marry me?

But I couldn't marry him. He wasn't a member of the Church.

Or could I?

It was eleven kinds of stupid to be thinking about that. But I had it on the best authority that teenage girls did this—I knew for a fact I wasn't the only one. What girl hadn't doodled her name mixed up with her boyfriend's last name?

Well, I hadn't done *that*, but I had thought about marrying Zack.

Before all this happened, I'd assumed I'd go to college, graduate, and perhaps work awhile before getting serious with a guy. But everything was different now. We were living like we were in the nineteenth century. Maybe our marriage customs ought to switch back to a younger age as well, like it was in the old days. It didn't seem so strange to imagine Zack and me sticking together through all the craziness, and when things got back to normal, we would return to Washington and work the Allman fields together . . . just the two of us . . .

My mind rocketed back to that day some seven or eight years ago when at church we were taught about being missionaries. I'd carried out my duty and invited Zack to Primary the next week.

Within the hour, Mr. Allman was on our front porch asking to speak to Dad and me. I'd hid halfway behind Dad's lanky frame as Mr. Allman had delivered his speech.

"Lee-Lee didn't mean anything by it, I'm sure," Mr. Allman had said. "But we'll be leaving off with church talk if that's okay with you. We've got our faith, and you've got yours. I've got no objection to these two kids being friends as long as we've got a deal on that." Mr. Allman's voice had been gruff, but he'd smiled to soften his words and had chucked me under the chin in a friendly way.

I'd wanted to be friends with Zack a hundred times more than I'd wanted to test Mr. Allman's patience on the Church thing, so I never invited Zack to anything else, and we avoided the topic from that time on.

Zack had brought it up just once a couple of years later. He'd mentioned his dad asked now and then if we were keeping our end of the deal. He'd told Zack to watch out because Mormons would do anything for a convert, including playing tricks on his mind, lying, or brainwashing him. We'd both laughed, but I'd felt a little sad that someone or something had spoiled it for Mr. Allman at some time in the past.

* * *

Zack stayed with our little group—Mom, me, Ethan, and Jarron—while he continued to heal.

At dinnertime, we sat eating the inevitable supper stew. These days, it seemed eating was more a chore rather than something to enjoy. Food Storage Goulash was getting really old.

A lady from one of the Yakima wards approached and squatted beside Mom. "Tina—we were wondering—it looks like Donna Harker is in labor, and we thought you might be able to help."

Mom jumped to her feet. "She's having her baby? Now? Are the doctors there?"

"No, they'll be along soon, I'm sure, but since it's her first baby, it's likely to take time. We thought you might know some things to make it go easier for her."

Mom's face lit up. "Sure! I'd love to lend a hand. Lee-Lee, why don't you come too?"

I stood hesitantly, looking at the boys.

"Don't look at us," Ethan said, holding his hands in front of him.

"We'll be fine right here," Jarron said.

I laughed. "No one expected you to help with a baby."

I followed Mom, who chattered happily with the Yakima sister about different herbal concoctions she'd used for birthing babies. I hadn't seen Mom this animated since—since Dad had left.

To my relief, Donna Harker wasn't in the middle of delivery when we arrived at her side. I knew childbirth was supposed to be a beautiful, natural event, but I didn't feel prepared to witness one that instant. The whole idea had always scared me, although I'd kept that fear to myself.

Donna, a young woman in her early twenties, looked remarkably normal. Not like TV show births, with loads of screaming and sweating. She sat on the ground, leaning against her husband, who looked a few shades paler than she did. Several other women sat nearby, and soon Mom and the rest were busily engaged in a discussion about how long and how far between. I hovered, waiting to be told to go boil water or something.

I thought about the pioneer stories and women having babies on the trail, with women holding blankets to keep off the rain and so on. At least it wasn't raining. Still, I couldn't imagine myself having a baby in this place. It sounded scary enough in a sterile hospital room with drugs and monitors all at the ready. I told myself that people have babies every day without those things, but I couldn't stop my heart from pounding when Donna's face squinched up.

Someone jotted the time down on a spiral notebook, and after only a few seconds, Donna relaxed again, laughing nervously. The women discussed this contraction's duration in relation to the last one and made pronouncements about how things were progressing.

Mom talked about various home remedies, most of which we didn't have with us. Nevertheless, it made me happy to see the women defer to her knowledge.

I found out they weren't kidding when they said first babies usually take a while. I fell asleep. Several hours later I awoke to Dr. Wilson's voice encouraging Donna. No screaming, but there was definitely effort involved. The baby was born under the dawn stars, and things seemed to go fine as far as I could tell. I saw very little beyond the clustered women standing near the actual birthing spot, but I did see the baby boy as gentle hands swiftly swaddled him. I heard his tiny cry, and I felt my spirit respond.

A minute ago, Donna was a young woman not so different from me—just a few years older. Now she was *a mother in Zion*. I'd heard that phrase so often its meaning almost didn't register; it was almost cliché. What did it mean now, now that everything was turned upside down? What would that child see? What would he need to be prepared for?

Then I looked at my own mother, her face beaming in a rare moment of acceptance and purpose among the other women. What will be my place, my life's work? A mother in Zion? Where is my Zion anymore?

* * *

Four days later, while Zack slipped off to find a necessary bush, I sat down under the pines lining the freeway and pulled out my sandwich. Right away, the missionaries—known in my mind as "the Ammon kid and the other one"—approached me.

"Hi, Elders," I said. "How are you holding out?"

"Not bad," Ammon—Elder Robertson, I read from his nametag—said. "Perhaps not as crisp and pressed as we once were, but we're hanging in there." We all laughed. They still wore white shirts and ties, although I guessed that was mostly because those were the only clothes they had, rather than any strict observance of mission rules.

"Pretty remarkable about your friend Zack," the other one said. A quick glance at his nametag reminded me he was really named Elder Shaw.

"Yes. Amazing. I can't believe he's okay."

"So that's the first time he's had a blessing, I'll bet," Elder Robertson said. "How do you think he felt about that?"

"He feels great about it. Wouldn't you?"

"Well, yes, of course. Just curious, though, if it's making him ask stuff about the Church."

"That's the big question, isn't it," I said. "Seems like everyone's asking it. But we've got to be real careful. His dad warned and warned him about pushy Mormons. I want it to be his idea. Don't bug him about it, okay?"

Zack walked up, looking from the missionaries to me. "Hi."

"Hey, Zack. How's it going? Looks like you're getting around real good," Elder Robertson said.

"Things are fine." Zack grinned and slung his arms across their shoulders. "You know, if you two were anyone else, I'd think you were hitting on Lee."

Elder Robertson barked out a short laugh. "Yeah, right. That'll have to wait."

Zack dropped his arms and folded them across his chest, but the grin didn't leave his face.

"So, uh, Zack—do you have any questions for us?"

"Questions? What about?"

What in the world were they doing? I made a cutting motion with my hands down where the missionaries could see but not Zack.

"About the Church." Elder Shaw grinned back, thumbing his nametag.

I wanted to scream. Had I not *just* told the missionaries to watch it? To wait and follow Zack's lead? To be careful? Now they were going to ruin everything. I shot daggers with my eyes at those idiot missionaries.

I opened my mouth, trying to think of some light comment. But before I could come up with anything, Elder Shaw interrupted me. "Elder Robertson and I were thinking you might like to sit down with us in the evenings and go through a series of little lessons about what we believe."

I felt my face flush red with embarrassment and anger. How dare they? How could this be salvaged? I frantically tried to think of how to smooth it over.

"Uh, okay. Sure," Zack said, shrugging.

I gaped at Zack. Could I have heard him correctly?

Elder Robertson winked at me. That really fried me. I was so furious I felt like jumping him and clawing his hair out. But I figured it would be best to act like it was no big deal, since that was the way Zack was taking it. Later I could see about damage control.

Besides, I *was* angry at the missionaries for disregarding my cautions, but at the same time, I was thrilled that Zack had actually agreed. I didn't dare think about what that might mean, what it might lead to.

I gave Elder Robertson the biggest crusty I could manage, and hooking my arm through Zack's, I stalked away, pulling him after me.

"See ya tonight, then," Elder Robertson called.

"'Kay," Zack called over his shoulder. "Should be fun," he said to me. "You can be there with me, right?"

"Sure," I said, trying to match his nonchalance.

"Remember, you promised to protect me from the big bad baptizers."

"Ha. Yeah. Right." I fought with everything I had not to show any emotion when I felt like crying a bucket of happy tears. "It'll be a good way to pass some time."

"Sister Hatch!" a voice called. I turned, and the bishop of the Sunnyside Ward approached.

"Yes?"

"Have you seen Ryan today?"

"Ryan Cook?"

"Yes. You're friends, right? He's in my company, and he didn't check in with me this morning like he usually does. Frankly, I'm worried, since I haven't seen him since yesterday."

"People do get spread out. And he told me he likes to get ahead of the group," I said.

"Yes, he does. I've tried to talk him out of that, but I obviously can't force him to stop. It's not safe. I hope he's okay. How about you, brother? Seen him around?"

Zack shook his head.

"Well, let me know if you see him."

I nodded, and the bishop moved on. I realized it had been at least a day or two since I'd seen that curly mop of Ryan's.

We walked. The road still sloped downward but not enough that it jarred my knees or made me stumble. The trees began to thin along the side of the road, and I felt a little sad when I remembered from past trips to Utah what the rest of the trip would be like. There were a few nice vistas to come, but for the most part, it would be a long straight road through nothing.

We walked roughly in the middle of the pack, and looking ahead, I was surprised to see the group bunching up. For some reason, the people in front had stopped. We were coming up on Baker City, so I wondered if there was a question about where to find its church. Couldn't be that hard. Baker was tiny.

I hoped with all my heart there wasn't a problem with using the meetinghouse in Baker. I'd been looking forward to staying at a church. It'd been ages since we'd been able to. There had been a church in La Grande a few days back, but with the trouble we'd had in Pendleton, the leaders had chosen to pass the town by.

I craved a shower. And real toilets, not skanky rest areas or a sagebrush. There was something comforting about the familiarity of the meeting-houses, and some of them even still had running water. In this part of the country, they were cookie-cutter—pretty much the same floor plan in each building. Their sameness was an anchor to hold on to.

"Wonder what's up," Zack said. We stepped through the press of people toward the front. When we got close enough, we could see a group of men ranged across the road, blocking our path. Rifles lay cradled across their arms.

More guns! I closed my eyes and shuddered.

President Green approached them and put his hand out to shake.

The apparent leader of the men didn't move. "You folks need to keep moving. Nobody's allowed into Baker."

"We're Mormons from up near Yakima," President Green said. "Just traveling through. We have a church in Baker we plan to use just overnight. Then we'll be out of your hair."

"We know who you are," the man replied. "But nobody's getting into Baker. We wouldn't let two Quakers in, much less two thousand Mormons. We don't mean to be unkind. But that's how it is."

"We've got our own food. There would be no drain on your resources."

"Sorry. We've had our troubles with out-of-towners, and we don't want more. You'll have to move out of this area."

President Green's shoulders sagged. "I understand. How about if we camp outside the town and we come in a few at a time to use our facility? Just to clean up? No one will bother you."

"Sorry. Baker's off limits."

It was plain from the men's resolute faces that we were getting nowhere near that Baker church building. I sighed, regretting the missed shower, but I couldn't blame them. Who knows what sort of trouble the town had already experienced? Bad folk were roaming the area, as we'd so painfully discovered.

"Come on; let's go," I said to Zack. "Might as well get a little ahead." I tried not to think about the fact that there was nothing, not even a town as small as Zillah, for the next sixty miles at least.

I wasn't the only one looking longingly at Baker as we passed. I even saw a couple of women in tears. The mood of the group turned from can-do to picked-on in only a few minutes.

"Give Mormons a challenge, and they'll tackle it. They jump right in. But get 'em complaining—look out," Zack said grimly as a couple of elders quorum presidents stomped by, bickering like fishwives.

"That's the gospel truth," I replied. "You caught on to us pretty quick."

The mountains gave way to puffy hills covered in mostly tree-barren rangeland. I noticed as I started down yet another hill that I could feel the road through the thinning soles of my shoes.

As usual, Zack had my backpack over one shoulder, his own over the other. As we walked, his left hand brushed my right one that clamped around the cane he'd made me. He patted it and smiled.

I'll have to contrive to get on the other side of him, I thought. *Then we could hold hands.*

Holding hands in public would be sort of an announcement that we were "together." Was I ready for that? I laughed at myself for having that question. Pretty funny, since at the same time I was plotting how to get him alone enough to kiss.

CHAPTER FOURTEEN

Monday, June 11

EVERYONE HAD BEEN READY TO stop in Baker, and now we had to gear ourselves up for a few more miles. The light was already fading, but we'd need to camp at least two or three miles out of town. On we shuffled.

Strange little thoughts started to creep into my mind. *This group needs cheering up.*

Yeah, so?

Everyone's tired and grumpy. You could help. You could make a difference.

Where were these thoughts coming from? After all, I was the queen of tired and grumpy.

Use your music. Tonight, when we camp. Lift their spirits.

I cringed. Like do what? Organize a sing-along? Would that help? I knew the old-timer pioneers used to do that.

And they used to dance.

My heart raced. A dance. It was exactly what this group needed. But how could it be done? And how could a cripple girl get it started?

I thought about what I knew of the pioneers. They'd cobble together a little band out of whatever instruments people happened to have, and off they'd go.

Well, I knew one person who had an instrument. Where was that dratted boy? I scanned the crowd for him like I'd done a hundred times already that day. He was nowhere in sight.

Thankfully, I found myself still fairly close to President Green. I caught up with him and ran the idea past him. He'd noticed the mood of the group as well and thought it a good idea. He even gave me names of people he thought likely to have brought an instrument.

I shivered. What was I starting? I wasn't a kid who felt comfortable putting herself out there. Give me the sidelines any day over the limelight. But the nagging feeling wouldn't leave. I plunged on.

Or, I should say, I got my brothers to plunge for me. I got them scurrying, talking to the people President Green had suggested. One had indeed brought a violin, another a trumpet, tucked away on a supply truck. Others had left their precious instruments at home but knew other people who'd brought theirs along.

When I ran out of leads, I had four violins, a trumpet, a flute, a guitar (not Ryan's), and, believe it or not, a banjo. Every one of them was flat-out excited about the prospect of playing for an impromptu hoedown. The combination of instruments was a bit odd, but who cared?

Pretty soon the musicians found each other and began hashing out ideas for songs as they walked. I found myself wishing, not for the first time, that I could play something a little more portable than a piano.

There was also a sad little wish that I could dance, but I quickly squashed that one.

The project took on a life of its own. News of the plans spread through the group, and people started to perk up. Relief washed over me. I'd done my little part to help, and it looked like I could fade into my favorite background spot.

"It's nice to see you smile again," Zack said.

"Was I smiling?"

"Yes, ma'am. Way to go, Lee-Lee. Good job."

When we were about four miles out of town, the leaders gave the signal to halt. People spread over the hillside to the side of the road, throwing out bedrolls and pulling cooking supplies from the trucks. I put my hands on my hips and looked around. Where would we dance? The hills were densely covered with sagebrush.

I looked down. The two ribbons of freeway stretched out to the north and south, with just a small median between, overgrown with long grasses. Right there on the road would be a great place. The chances of a vehicle coming along were small. At this point, a car or truck went by only once every three or four days, our group parting to the sides of the road to let them pass.

* * *

President Green spoke to the group nearly every night after supper, sometimes a longer exhortation but often nothing more than a short blessing. He'd agreed to announce the dance this evening, provided I talk to each of the captains to give them a heads-up.

That was scary, approaching these busy men, telling them about a dumb little dance—one more thing to worry about. But each one seemed kind and solicitous toward me. I discovered I had a bit of notoriety as "the poor girl who got kidnapped." Everyone seemed to know my name—not just "the Hatch girl" as I might have been to people from far-flung wards.

I was nearly too nervous to eat supper. I wanted the dance to be fun, a step away from everyone's cares. I also didn't want to look like a big dummy for dreaming it up. I was staring at my half-eaten bowl of stew when President Green gave the word.

The musicians gathered, tuning their instruments, and an excited hum spread through the group when they began playing "Turkey in the Straw." I watched the people's faces. They looked interested but hesitant.

No one started dancing. My heart sank.

I knew the best thing to do would be to step out and start dancing—to get the ball rolling. But I couldn't do that.

Or could I?

I looked at Zack standing beside me. The blessed boy read my mind.

"Let's get this party started." He held his hands out to me.

"How?" I whispered.

"Step on my boots and hang on. I'll do the rest."

I laid down my cane.

I gingerly stepped onto Zack's feet. He put his right arm around my back and took my other hand in his. I had no time to think about how nice it was to be so close to him before he started moving to the music, slowly at first and then faster as we caught on to the idea.

I laughed out loud in spite of the embarrassment of every single person in the stake looking at me. I was dancing! And almost immediately, people young and old started dancing all around us, on the asphalt freeway in the middle of Nowhere, Oregon.

We danced that way for a few songs, then I heard a distinct change in the music. Suddenly, it sounded fuller, richer, with an unmistakable string-picking pattern that wove in and out of the other instruments' chords.

My head snapped around. I knew even before I saw him. Ryan was back and had joined in with the little band.

"Let's take a break," I said to Zack. "Your poor feet need rest." I sat down where I could see Ryan's hands. I caught his eye, and he grinned and winked.

Where had Ryan been all this time? Curiosity ate me up, but for the moment, all I wanted to do was watch him play.

"He's amazing, isn't he?" Zack said beside me.

"Mm-hmm." I nodded.

I listened, transfixed, for a song or two. Then I tore my eyes away and looked around the crowd, hoping to ascertain if people were having a good time.

It looked like nearly everyone was enjoying themselves, even the kids. I noticed only two people sitting to the side with glum looks on their faces. The missionaries.

"Oh, Zack, look at those poor guys," I said, pointing them out.

"What's wrong with them?"

"Well, I guess they're bummed because everyone's having fun dancing, but they can't. They're not allowed."

"Oh. Hmm," Zack replied. "Want to go talk to them? Cheer them up?"

I nodded, and as we worked our way over to where they sat, I realized they might be gloomy because their teaching appointment for the evening had been caught up in other stuff. Our appointment.

Sure enough, when we approached, Elder Robertson's face lit up. "Hey! How are ya?"

"Good," Zack replied. "So missionaries can't dance, eh? Seems pretty harmless."

"Yeah. Well, there will be plenty of time for that when we get off our missions. If the world hasn't blown up by then."

"We're really looking forward to talking with you," Elder Shaw said. "Think we can still fit that in tonight?"

"Sure," Zack replied. "Let me dance one more time with Lee, and then we'll come right back." He put his arm around me and grinned at the missionaries. "That cool with you guys?" He swept his arm behind my legs and picked me up. I squeaked in surprise.

"What are you doing, weirdo?" I demanded as he strode off toward the dance area.

"I've been wanting to do that since this walk-to-Utah insanity started," he said, that grin still plastered across his face.

I pretended to act affronted, but I had to admit, I liked being in his arms.

Zack marched right in front of the musicians, and I saw him glance at Ryan. Up until that moment, Zack had seemed oblivious of my friendship with Ryan. But the look on Zack's face showed he was anything but unaware and was making a statement of his own.

He spun around a couple of times until I laughed with giddy dizziness. He set me gently down, and I stepped onto his boots like I had before. His arm across my back pressed me close.

As we danced, I stole a peek at Ryan. I couldn't tell if he'd noticed us, since his head was tipped down over the blur of his enchanted fingers.

The song ended, and Zack picked me up again.

"Honestly, Zack, I feel ridiculous."

"Just trying to save a little time. Those missionaries are chomping at the bit." We arrived back where they sat, and Zack deposited me on a handy log.

Elder Shaw smiled a little wistfully. "That dancing looked fun."

"Oh, it was," Zack said.

"So, Zack, Elder Robertson and I were talking—wondering how much you know about our faith. Has Sister Hatch told you quite a bit?"

"Actually, no. My father forbade us to discuss it."

"He did? Uh . . . but now . . ."

"He's dead."

Elder Shaw flushed. "Oh. I'm sorry."

An awkward silence stretched out until Elder Robertson broke in. "Sister Hatch, what have you been wishing the most for Zack to know about our faith?"

That question set me back. There were a hundred things. What was the most? I sent up a quick prayer. What did God want him to know the most?

"I guess I'd want him to know that God's really there and knows him," I said.

"How would he learn that?"

I searched my heart for the memory of when that had happened to me. "Do you guys still have a Book of Mormon with you?"

"Sure." Elder Shaw reached into his backpack and pulled out the familiar blue-covered book.

"Can I write in this?" I asked. Elder Robertson nodded and handed me the book and a pen. "For me, it was all about this book. I'm sure it happens differently for each person. But as soon as I knew this book was true, the other answers fell into place." I flipped it open to Alma 32 and circled a few verse numbers. Then I underlined the promise at the end of Moroni. I handed the book to Zack.

I'm sure the earth shifted at that moment, when Zack's fingers closed around the book.

Zack looked at me steadily. I searched his face but couldn't tell if he could sense the electric charge surging through the air. I did my best to look casual while I strove to keep from jumping up and down.

"I'll read it. The priest wouldn't approve, but I suppose I can beg forgiveness later. Let's see what all the fuss is about."

We arranged to meet with the missionaries again on Monday night. It was late, so we crossed the camp to our bedrolls.

Mom and the boys were already asleep. Zack always put his roll in a discreet place on the other side of my brothers, not too far away. I said my prayers and watched his face in the silvery moonlight from my spot two arm lengths away. The soft fingers of sleep smoothed away the lines of care and worry around his eyes, and I fell into dreams of walking, walking, walking.

Finally Sunday came. Never had a day of rest held so much meaning. Sacrament meeting seemed strange, sitting on the ground, but, honestly, what was strange and what was normal anymore?

President Green seemed sober. As usual, he thanked us, praised us, and encouraged us. But his responsibility seemed to weigh heavy. Perhaps it had something to do with the ham radio message from Salt Lake City he'd shared with us. Apparently, reestablishing order wasn't going too well for the government. I felt a shiver of fear, thinking once again about what the cities would be like in this chaos.

* * *

Monday morning held more hills, more scattered farms and ranches. When I had driven this road before, there were always lots of cows grazing those fields. Now I didn't see a single animal. I wondered if the ranchers kept them close at hand for safety or if bad guys had taken them.

A sluggish creek flowed beside the freeway, and Jarron and Ethan, along with several other kids, enjoyed walking right in the cold water. I knew from school that this area was near the original Oregon Trail, and with all the water and green hills, it was easy to see why so many pioneers had made it their destination.

Not our destination though. We were making our own Mormon Trail.

I eagerly looked around for Ryan. I'd been so happy to see him back, safe and sound, last night at the dance, but there'd been no time to say anything. I wanted to find him to know where he'd been. It certainly didn't look like there was anything interesting to look at in the hills surrounding our path, so it was hard to believe he'd been here.

What would it be like to be able to run and run with no pain or awkwardness? To be able to take off and go exploring and still be able to catch up with the group when you'd had your fix? It was all I could do to keep one step ahead of the green truck.

As usual, I'd started off early and was in the front of the pack, but people gradually passed me. I'd watched for him, but no Ryan. By lunchtime, it was obvious he wasn't with the group anymore. I frowned in frustration. I felt a prick of sadness that he hadn't felt compelled to search me out and say hello. Or good-bye. Why did I keep looking for him? Why did I care? That boy was just plain annoying and nothing else.

I kept one eye on Zack, watching his expression. He walked with the Book of Mormon open in his hands, held up in front of his face. I burned with curiosity to know what he thought of it but didn't dare bug him.

At supper, the choices were rice and black beans or rice and pinto beans. One scoop each, no more. I thought back longingly to the food storage goulash I'd so recently complained about. Jarron and Ethan ate silently for the whole five minutes it took to clean their plates. I tried to imagine them eating a meal like that a month ago. They would have whined to high heaven. Now, we ate what we were given with only one thought: would the boxes and bags of food storage hold out? We'd already consolidated the cargo trucks a few times as they'd emptied. Only ten remained out of fifteen, the empty trucks abandoned on the roadside.

After dinner, Zack and I once again sat with the missionaries at one of the fire pits.

"So how's the reading going?" Elder Robertson asked.

Zack's face was inscrutable. "Okay. It's not that easy to read, you know."

"Oh yeah, I know. Lots of people get bogged down in 2 Nephi when it starts quoting Isaiah."

"Oh, is that how you say it? I was saying *Ne-fee* in my head." Zack laughed. "It's one freaky book."

My heart sank a little. So much for hopes of "I was gripped by the Spirit and stayed up all night reading it, and can I be baptized, please?"

The missionaries gave their little lesson. They talked about God, the Atonement, family, etc., etc. It was all so familiar to me that I had to wonder if it was to Zack as well. Pretty basic Christian-type stuff.

I watched Zack carefully as the lesson progressed to an explanation of the Reformation. How would he react to this information as a Catholic? His face was a blank slate as the missionaries described the Apostasy and subsequent inspired works of Luther, Calvin, and so on. Zack appeared to be taking it all in but made no comment.

And then they told the story of Joseph Smith's First Vision, and I felt my mouth dry out with nervousness. Gold plates! Visions! Angels! How would all of that sound to Zack? Since I'd grown up with it, it seemed as normal as sunshine in the morning, but to someone else, it had to sound downright odd. Still, the warmth of the Spirit permeated my soul, as it always did when I heard the story of the young Prophet. Could Zack feel it? It seemed so strong.

He finally spoke. "Okay, that's really weird," he said. "You guys actually believe that stuff?"

"I know it sounds different," Elder Shaw said, "but is it really so much stranger than what you read in the Bible? I mean, how about a talking donkey and plagues of frogs?"

"Wait—there's a talking donkey in the Bible?"

"Yep."

"The Mormon Bible though, right?"

"We use the King James Version, which I believe is the same as the one used in the Catholic Church."

"Huh. Okay. Whatever you say."

Elder Shaw offered a prayer, and after the amens, the missionaries rose to their feet. "Thanks for letting us teach the gospel again. That was nice for us," Elder Shaw said. "See ya tomorrow?"

"Sure." Zack shrugged. They walked away to their bedrolls, leaving us alone at the fire pit.

"At last," Zack said with a smile, putting his arms around me.

I slipped my arms around his neck. "Sorry—it seems like you got a lot of weird stuff dumped on you all at once."

"It's okay."

"Why are you doing this, Zack? With the missionaries, I mean? Because of your miracle?"

Zack put on a devilish grin. "Everyone says if you're not a Mormon, you can't get anywhere with a Mormon girl."

"Zack!"

"What I mean is—you can't get serious with a Mormon girl. Isn't that right?"

"Yeah, I suppose so," I mumbled. "If she's a good Mormon girl."

"And you are. And that's what I want. To get serious with one."

I pulled back a little so I could look into his eyes that flickered with firelight. I searched his familiar face—where I'd seen every kind of happy and sad, where I'd seen his round boyish cheeks sprinkled with freckles grow up. "When we were kids, did you ever see us getting together?"

"I always hoped."

"You did? Always?"

"From the time we were little. I could never picture anyone but you."

"Even when I beat you at Battleship?"

"Even."

"How about when you put a snake in the piano?"

"Showing my devotion."

I wondered for an instant if that stuff he'd said about getting serious with a Mormon girl meant he was willing to discard his family's faith for me. A flicker of worry dashed through my mind. After all, for a Mormon girl, it had to be real. He couldn't fake the Mormon thing, if that's what he was saying he planned to do.

Then I felt his arms gently tighten around my shoulders, and thought and reason left me.

CHAPTER FIFTEEN

Thursday, June 21

THE NEXT FEW DAYS WENT by in a blur of happiness. The days, of course, were filled with walking across hills and more hills, but the landscape gradually flattened out again. We crossed into Idaho, which made me think this never-ending journey might actually end someday and we might really get to Utah.

We spent the evenings talking to the missionaries and trying to catch a moment or two of privacy. With so many people around, that wasn't easy.

Was Zack really getting it? I couldn't tell. During our talks with the missionaries, he didn't say much. He'd just sit there with his arms folded across his chest. I didn't know too much about body language, but he looked less than eager. He answered direct questions but otherwise stayed politely quiet. The missionaries tried to warm him up, joshed around with him, acted buddy-buddy. But Zack kept it businesslike, and the missionaries ended up making the lessons pretty short, maybe fifteen minutes or so each.

He still read the Book of Mormon during the day, but he wasn't exactly blazing through it. I didn't know what to think.

During one of the rare moments Zack wasn't walking beside me, Sherry, a girl my age whom I vaguely knew, fell into step.

"How's your boyfriend doing, Amélie?" she asked. "I heard he's taking the missionary lessons."

"I think it's going pretty well." I smiled at her. I knew she was talking to me only because she was curious about Zack, but that was no excuse for me to be snotty. And the fact that she called Zack my boyfriend made my insides tingle. Was he my boyfriend? I supposed he was. He seemed to meet the boyfriend test. Did we like each other? Holy cow yes. Were we exclusive—only seeing each other? Yes. Did we kiss and hold hands? When we could. Pass 100 percent.

Amélie has a boyfriend! I felt like singing the words at the top of my voice. I had to admit, I'd wondered if it would ever happen. I'd see people together and think that sort of thing was not for me. Not for a screwup with a bum leg and a chip on her shoulder.

Maybe I wasn't as much of a disaster as I'd always thought.

The only thing disturbing my budding happiness was my concern for Ryan. I didn't know what to think about the fact that he still hadn't come back. Even the leaders, who had shrugged at his capriciousness before, were concerned. During one of President Green's nightly announcement sessions, he asked everyone to watch for him. There wasn't much more we could do.

It'd been days and days. Where was he sleeping? It wasn't that cold out, but the thought of him sleeping alone somewhere made me squirm with nervousness. There weren't just wild animals in this bleak, deserted country; there were wild people too. Wild, desperate people.

Plus, I doubted Ryan knew how to take care of himself. Sure, he had an independent spirit and didn't seem timid or uncertain, but had he ever had to defend himself? Forage for food? I doubted it. It seemed more likely that he'd had everything handed to him up until now.

As we moved farther into Idaho, the land around the freeway became more and more urban. There were plenty of churches to stay in, at least, but I wondered what it would be like to walk down a freeway bisecting a city as big as Boise. The area held over a half million people. I shuddered to think about the challenges those people must have encountered over the last month. It was one thing to do without power on a farm with plenty of food and water at hand. It was another thing altogether for people who lived in a city. How were they managing? Was there any kind of order at all? How could we safely take our precious supplies through?

We pulled in, footsore and exhausted, to a church in Nampa. I noticed the placard in front of the church that announced its name as the Nampa East Stake Center. Did that mean there was more than one stake in Nampa? Wow. That's a lot of Mormons in one place, and this wasn't even Utah.

When I walked into the gym, I noticed immediately that something was different. I was used to being one of the last to arrive, and often dinner preparations were well underway before I got there. But this time, things seemed even more ready than normal. The tables were set up nicely and were actually spread with white butcher paper, like they do for ward dinners. Food adorned a few serving tables under the basketball hoops, and although I couldn't see yet what the ladies had prepared, it smelled delicious. It smelled like something besides beans. Hungry trekkers already stood in a queue, plates in hand.

Before I finished wondering what the occasion was, I noticed unfamiliar faces manning the serving tables. Mom and the boys stood toward the end of the line, so I hurried over to them.

"Who are those people?" I asked.

"Oh, they're folks from the Nampa East Stake," Mom replied. "Isn't it nice? They made dinner for us. A few days ago, they heard we were on the road and decided to help out by setting all this up." She sighed happily. "How nice to walk in, all tuckered out, and have a nice dinner all ready for us. These people are nice. Very nice. What nice people."

"Wow," I said. "Wonderful!"

When we reached the serving tables, Mom went around and hugged the lady scooping mashed potatoes. "You guys don't know what this means to us," she gushed. "All of you. You're angels." As usual, she got teary.

The lady smiled and looked at the others serving with her. "When we found out you were headed our way, we had to do something to help. Glad you like it."

Pretty soon everybody was wiping away tears. I looked at the serving women. They looked kind, a bit careworn, and quite ordinary. Two had the requisite granny 'fros. I'd never seen these women before, but there was something so familiar about them. I finally decided the commonality lay behind their eyes. We all had the gospel, and that spirit created an instant bond. I hoped the same thing would happen once we reached Utah.

I couldn't help wondering how they'd managed to put on this spread. Food supplies had to be tight. I opened my mouth to ask and then closed it again. They were sharing food that logic said they should be hoarding, and that made the gift feel sacred. It felt wrong to quiz them about it.

I even heard a couple of people saying they thought they'd just stay right there in Nampa and never mind about going the rest of the way to Utah. But that wouldn't be right. Not when their supplies were so tight. We had to keep going.

* * *

When we left Nampa, I discovered the men of the Nampa East Stake had their own gift. More than a hundred armed men marched on our flanks. They guided us through Boise, picking up more Mormon men to join their ranks as we went. We'll never know what harassment we might have received without them, but no one wanted to bother a group like ours, hedged with men bristling with weapons. As soon as we reached the southern outskirts, the men returned to their homes.

Once again, the road became an arrow through a bleak, empty landscape. The heat of summer was brutal. No shelter. No shade. I spent the day longing for sundown and was grateful when it finally came.

All the next day, Zack seemed strangely preoccupied as we walked. He was usually so great with Ethan and Jarron, but today he hardly responded to their kidding and chatter. He still held his Book of Mormon but only fingered it restlessly. I kept catching him looking at me—practically staring. Efforts to start a conversation fell flat.

I couldn't wait until evening when we'd meet with the missionaries and then have some private time to talk afterward. Those moments had quickly become my favorite part of the day, and looking forward to it kept me going when the road got hard.

Something was eating at Zack. I fretted that he'd read something bothersome but he was afraid to tell me. Fear fluttered at the bottom of my stomach. What was wrong?

Finally the time arrived for our meeting with the missionaries. Zack seemed pensive. The missionaries gave their brief discussion and, perhaps picking up on his quiet mood, wrapped things up quickly. As soon as they left the fire pit, I turned to Zack, anxious to find out the trouble.

To my surprise, he stood up. I reached out to catch his hand to pull him back beside me. He stepped back, and my hand closed on nothing. I stared at him in alarm.

"Lee, I've been trying to figure out how to say this all day. There's no good way. I'm just going to blurt it out."

His face was a picture of misery. What in the world was going on?

"I gotta break up with you, Lee. It isn't working."

"What?" My heart hit my toes. I felt like I'd been struck. "What do you mean?"

"Just what I said." Zack put a hand over his eyes for a moment, and I saw his Adam's apple bob as he swallowed. "I don't want to talk about it. I need you to just drop it."

And just like that, he turned on his heel and walked away, leaving me sitting there on a log, completely blown away. For five long minutes, I couldn't speak, move, think, nothing. Then I cried. What happened? What did I do? Those two questions repeated over and over in my mind, and there was no answer.

* * *

When I woke up bleary-eyed the next morning, I prayed that what Zack had told me was only a dream. But the dawn had a sharp relentlessness about it, baring everything to the sky, uncovering my grief and shock in its starkness. I buried my head under my pillow, pressing my face against the hard ground. It was true. It had really happened. Zack had rejected me.

I'd lost my love, my best friend. My only friend.

My mind recirculated all of the bad thoughts I'd dwelt on the entire night. I must have done something, said something. I shouldn't have pressed my religion on him. I was funny looking. I annoyed him. I was broken.

It was a miracle he ever cared for me. I'm pathetic.

I wallowed in that for a few minutes but finally hauled myself out of my sleeping bag.

I looked around the stirring camp. I didn't see Zack. He hadn't slept near us last night. I had no idea where he'd ended up rolling out his bag. I forced myself to stop searching the crowd for him.

I went through the motions of eating breakfast and packing to leave. I felt like an automaton, my hands moving in practiced patterns without much thought. Everything felt dull and gray.

Then Zack's words floated back, sparking a fresh round of weeping. I wished for the sodden detachment I'd felt a moment ago.

"What's wrong, Lee-Lee?" Ethan asked as we moved out onto the road. Jarron and Mom perked up.

Drat. "You weren't supposed to notice," I blubbered. I knew there was no point in hiding the truth from my family. After all, they'd surely notice Zack's absence. "Zack broke up with me. But I'm okay. Really, I am."

"Why'd he do that?"

"I don't know." I shrugged and forced a smile, putting my arm across Ethan's shoulder so he'd know everything was fine.

"Aw, honey," Mom said. She patted my shoulder. "The first love's the hardest—"

"I'm gonna walk by myself for a while," I broke in hurriedly. I knew what was coming from Mom. She'd give an in-depth dissertation on getting in touch with my feelings, and that was the last thing I wanted. I wanted to cut my feelings right out of my heart. I hoped she wasn't too hurt as I moved to the side of the road to walk.

Thankfully, they decided to let me have my space for a while. I stumped along, wiping my wet cheeks, ignoring the curious looks from the other people passing by.

For the thousandth time, I went over the last conversation between Zack and me. When had things transformed from perfect to horrible? I couldn't think of anything that could have caused a sudden change.

There probably wasn't something specific. He probably just got grossed out.

* * *

Three, maybe four awkward days passed with the two of us avoiding each other, not speaking, trying to be as far away from each other as possible.

On the fifth day since the breakup, I looked over my shoulder, and there he was, walking alone about fifty feet behind me. When our eyes caught, he quickly looked down. I stopped walking, my heart pounding.

"We're going to have this out," I muttered.

One side of my brain cried out, *Leave him alone! Don't say anything! Turn around and walk.* But my legs wouldn't move. *Do you want to look like you're begging? After the way he's treated you, he doesn't deserve you.* I stared at him as he came closer. He didn't try to move out of my path—he looked resigned, like someone trudging off to a dreaded chore.

He stopped in front of me and slowly raised his eyes. He looked miserable. I knew I looked worse—my eyes had to be red and my face blotchy. I dabbed at a little sweat on my forehead with my sleeve.

"I'm sorry, Lee," he said, his voice tight and strained. "I really don't want to talk about it."

"Zack, we've been friends since we were babies. Don't you think I deserve some explanation?" I hated how my voice caught and sounded quivery. "At least tell me what it was I did wrong. For training purposes."

"It was nothing you did, okay? Nothing."

"Then what happened?"

"Someday, I hope I'll be able to explain. Someday I hope you'll forgive me. But please, Lee. I'm asking you to just let it go. I'm sorry." This time he didn't just turn and walk away; this time he actually jogged away, knowing there was no way I could follow.

"Jerk," I said, but not quite loud enough for him to hear.

* * *

It goes without saying that we stopped meeting with the missionaries. I don't know if Zack cancelled with them or not. I sure didn't.

"If you want to talk, honey, I'm here," Mom said as we rolled out our sleeping bags.

"Okay. Thanks." I climbed in and pulled the bag over my head. I hoped prayers could pierce through a sleeping bag because I was not getting out. Maybe ever.

I lay in a haze of almost sleep for hours, listening to the night sounds of the desert and trying to layer a protective coating on my bruised heart. But *it isn't working* just kept hammering in my head. What wasn't working?

A rustle beside me startled me into alertness.

"Pssst! Amélie!"

I jumped as I felt a hand lightly cover my mouth. It felt like a man's hand, large and callused.

"Shhh. It's okay. It's me."

Fear coursed through me. A man's form crouched beside me. Then I relaxed as the voice registered as harmless, as it registered as a friend's. For a moment, I thought maybe it was Zack, come to set things right. Then the smooth voice whispering in my ear clicked with recognition.

Not Zack. Ryan.

CHAPTER SIXTEEN

Tuesday, July 3

I STARED AT HIM, HIS handsome features enhanced by moonlight. "What on earth are you doing?" I whispered. "You scared me to death! Where have you been?"

He set a finger to his lips. "Don't worry about it. Come with me. I've got a surprise for you."

"Come with you? Where?"

"Just outside camp. Shhh! Pretend like you're up for the bathroom. I'll meet you behind the latrine." He ghosted away into the dark.

Go with him? At first I laughed at the idea. Then the thought of an adventure—with Ryan Cook, no less—grew until I found myself crawling out of my sleeping bag.

Sensible Amélie chattered anxiously in my head. *You've got to be crazy. If you get caught sneaking out of camp with a boy in the middle of the night . . . think how that will look . . . what will people think . . . what would Zack think . . .*

Adventurous Amélie retorted, *I don't care what Zack would think.*

That was a lie, but lying to yourself didn't really count, did it? Zack had hurt me badly, and the fact that a way cute boy wanted my company made the whole thing irresistible. Just what my ego needed.

I shivered with nervousness as I stepped behind the latrine where Ryan waited. Getting caught would be so horribly embarrassing. I couldn't believe I was doing this.

"How are we going to get past the sentries?" I whispered. "Ever since the thing in Pendleton, they've really beefed that up."

"No problem." Ryan grinned. "I've snuck in and out of camp plenty of times. I know right where the sleepy high priests are posted. Just follow me."

Sure enough, we walked right out of camp. No one stirred; no one challenged us. My heart thudded against my ribs until we were well past the supply trucks.

We topped a small rise. How weird it felt to look back on the camp. I hadn't been outside its circle since the journey began, except when I'd been kidnapped.

We walked about a mile. I couldn't see anything but sagebrush for quite some distance. There might have been a farmhouse off to the left, but I couldn't see much in the moonlit night.

"Where are we going?" I puffed.

"Almost there. I can't wait for you to see your surprise."

Worry flickered through my mind. I thought I knew Ryan well enough to trust him to behave like a gentleman, but he seemed to be leading me off into nothing. Why would he bring me out here?

"Here it is." Ryan scampered ahead to an extra-large sagebrush nearly as tall as he was. He began pulling on something big nestled under its branches.

My mouth dropped open. "A motorcycle?"

Ryan was so excited he nearly danced. "Ain't it great? When I saw it, the first thing I thought of was you. Each night, we could sneak out and ride it to the next camp. Then we can lollygag the whole day while everyone else catches up. Then it won't be . . . so hard for you."

Stunned, I groped for words. "Wow. It's nice of you to think of me. But that would feel like cheating somehow. And we really should give this motorcycle to the leaders. They could use it to help patrol."

"Aw, come on. They don't need it."

"You can get away with sneaking out of camp, Ryan, but it'd never work for me. What a ruckus that would cause! Besides, I gotta walk, just like everyone else."

Zack would have understood that.

"At least take me for a ride. Wouldn't it be fun to really go fast for a change?"

I remembered how I used to go out in the Bluebird for exactly that reason. It was a miracle I'd never been pulled over. Speeding down the country highways made me feel free of my chains for a little while.

"Wait . . . you said 'take *me* for a ride.'"

"Yeah, uh, pretty embarrassing, but I don't have a clue how to ride it myself. I figured you farm kids know all about motorcycles though. You know how, right?"

"Sure. But how did you get it here if you didn't ride it?"

"I pushed it."

"From where?" I looked around the dark countryside.

"There's an abandoned farm just over that rise. I found it there. Come on, Amélie. Teach me how to ride it. Let's play with it for a little while, and then we can give it to the leaders if that's what you want."

So that's why he wanted to take me somewhere alone in the dark. My motorcycle know-how. It made sense it would be something like that instead of my stunning beauty.

Still, as long as I was out here, I supposed we could have a little fun with it. There were worse things in the world than hanging out with Ryan Cook.

"Okay," I said. "It's not that hard. As long as the thing will start." I laid my cane under the same bush where the bike had been hidden.

"The key was in it," Ryan said. "That's good, right?"

I laughed. "Yeah, that's good."

He held it upright while I threw a leg over and kicked the starter. After a couple of tries, it sputtered to life. The engine sounded frighteningly loud, echoing across the empty desert. Could they hear it all the way back at camp?

"Hop on," I shouted over the roar. Ryan climbed on behind me and put his arms around my middle. Janie Siddoway would never believe it if she saw me now.

I eased the throttle open, and soon we bounced across the desert, swooping back and forth between the sagebrush, visible in the bright moonlight. My hair streamed out behind me, blowing in Ryan's face, so he nestled his head next to mine. I laughed out loud. I'd forgotten how fun it was to go fast. Having Ryan so near, scrunched up behind me with his arms tight around, was a bonus I could live with.

I aimed away from camp, wanting to get the racket of the engine farther away from the guards.

I am going to get in so much trouble. And I don't care. Not right now. I'll worry about that later. I forced away thoughts of Zack and what he'd think of this.

"Hey, what's that?" Ryan asked in my ear. He pointed to a large dark form on the ground.

"Let's go find out." I turned the bike in that direction, and we zoomed over to the object.

"Whoa!" I breathed out.

We pulled to a stop, and I killed the engine. There, in front of us, was the hulking carcass of a downed four-seater aircraft. It hadn't come down too hard, although the landing gear was all messed up and it leaned against one wing.

"Must have got caught in the EMP," I said.

"I'll check for, uh, bodies," Ryan said, climbing onto the nose to peer through the windshield. "Too dark. Can't see anything." He clambered over to the door and wrenched it open. He disappeared inside.

His head popped back out. "No one. They must have been okay and walked somewhere."

I looked around the ground and could see trails of matted sage and cheat grass. Something heavy had been dragged away from the airplane.

"I can't see much in the dark, but it looks like they dragged something off," I said. "Maybe someone's hurt, and we should try to follow the tracks. Although I guess it'll be pretty hard to look in the dark."

"It'll be lighter soon," Ryan said.

I looked up in alarm at the eastern horizon. The sky was indeed beginning to purple. I realized I had no idea what time it was when we'd left camp or even how long we'd been gone. *Busted.*

"Oh no," I groaned. "I am so toast."

"We've gotta find out if someone needs our help," Ryan said. "Let's follow the tracks as best we can. Looks like they're headed for that farmhouse." He pointed eastward, where a house and farm outbuildings were silhouetted against the lightening sky. I started the bike again, and we took off in that direction.

When we were about two hundred yards away, I stopped. "You know, maybe we shouldn't go charging right up to the door making all this noise. If there's someone awake at that house, they've already heard us, but let's go quietly the rest of the way. How do we know what kind of people we'll find? Let's look around, see what's up, before talking to anyone."

Ryan shrugged. "Okay. I guess a few more minutes won't matter."

We hid the bike and set off walking. The drag marks led straight to the house. Had someone died in the crash and the survivors dragged the body here? Or maybe they'd dragged someone too hurt to walk? I shuddered to think what a painful trip that might have been.

I had to cling to Ryan's arm as we walked on cat's feet across the lawn surrounding the house. Candlelight flickered behind one of the windows. Someone was awake in the house.

"Well, look there." I pointed to an old truck parked to the side of the house. "That thing's old enough to still work." We crept into the bushes planted below the front window.

We were just getting ready to peep through the window when the screen door banged open like it had been pushed with a foot. My heart jumped into my throat.

"Hurry up!" a man's voice hissed in a clipped English accent. "You heard that noise. We've waited too long as it is. We've got to get this out of here *now*!"

Two men, one fair-haired and the other dark, struggled out the front door, maneuvering a bulky dolly—like one you'd use to move a refrigerator—over the threshold. It held a fifty-five gallon drum. I watched, petrified, as the men passed right next to our hiding place. They eased the dolly down the front steps with exaggerated care. What was in that drum? Gasoline? I supposed a person might be afraid gas would combust, but their motions seemed too extreme for the drum to be holding gas.

There was a little control box fastened to the top of the drum. Peering closer through the branches, I saw the box held a switch with colored wires leading from it. I'd seen enough James Bond movies. It looked like a bomb.

One man got into the old truck and backed it up to the end of the front walk. Leaving it running, he got out, put the tailgate down, and laid a board against it, forming a ramp. The other pushed the dolly up and into the bed of the pickup, swearing a hot British streak the whole way.

"Strap it down tight. I'm not having a nuke bouncing around loose all the way to Ogden," the first man said.

I sucked in a gasp, and Ryan's hand tightened on my arm. My heart hammered. A nuke! Ogden! I knew there was an air force base there. Every time we'd driven to Utah for family vacations, Dad had pointed it out as we passed Ogden on our way to Salt Lake City.

The men draped a tarp over the drum and fiddled with bungee cords until it was tied down tightly. "Have you got the remote?" the second man asked.

"Of course."

These men didn't sound like terrorist types, although in the faint light, I thought the dark-haired man looked foreign. I thought fleetingly of how I'd misjudged the Hispanic group.

I had no doubt if they found us hiding, they'd kill us.

"Bring out the gas cans and fill the truck. I'll carry Jacque out. He shouldn't be moved, but we have no choice." The men headed back into the house.

"To the truck! Run for it!" Ryan hissed.

It took me only a moment to catch on. Ryan meant to take the truck, bomb and all, to keep it from being delivered to a target in Utah.

I couldn't run, but I hobbled as fast as I ever had. I ripped open the passenger door while Ryan got into the driver's seat. The second my bottom hit the seat, he jammed the gas pedal to the floor.

"Keep down!" Ryan yelled over the roar of the engine. "They'll come after us. And they'll be shooting."

I managed to get the door shut as the truck bounced wildly down a gravel road.

"I hope this connects to the freeway somewhere," I gasped. Ryan shifted, and my body flattened against the seat back as the truck surged forward.

"It's got to." Ryan tossed a glance over his shoulder. "Here they come!"

The two men burst from the house. They took off running, one of them bringing a rifle to his shoulder. I prayed he was a terrible shot. We were well within rifle range, although Ryan was putting some good distance between us.

A bullet hit the back end, maybe the tailgate. I stifled a scream. What would happen if they hit the bomb?

I tried to reason with myself that nothing would happen. But I wasn't capable of reason. I couldn't breathe.

Ryan swerved the truck back and forth. I guessed that was partly to make us harder to hit and partly because it was hard to drive hunkered down like he was.

Bullets hit the truck a few more times. One struck the corner of the back window, scaring me half to death. The glass broke into a million little pieces and rained down, covering the seat. I peeked over the seat back and saw the small forms of the men in the distance. Maybe they were still following us, but they'd stopped shooting.

Ryan still had the accelerator jammed to the floor, his face a rigid mask and his long fingers curled into clamps on the steering wheel. Ahead, the gravel road turned to pavement and led to an on-ramp to the freeway.

"Should we take this thing to the camp?" he asked. "Is that wise?"

"What else could we do with it? Dismantle it or something?"

"Are you crazy? What if it blew up?"

"It's not dynamite." My words sounded brave, but I shivered at the thought of touching the bomb.

"We're not gonna try to dismantle it. We're not messing with it *at all*," Ryan said through his teeth. "I wonder how far we can get. The gauge is below *E*. We'll have to find gas."

As we pulled onto the freeway, the truck hiccupped and sputtered.

"Not very far," I said, trying to keep the tremble out of my voice. "Remember they said they needed to fill up the truck? They'll know we ran out of gas right away." The engine caught one more time and then died.

Ryan slammed the steering wheel with his palm. "We only got a couple of miles. They'll be here quick. We've gotta get out of here. We have to hide, stay alive somehow! We've got to warn people. Oh, man—I don't wanna die!" He jumped out of the truck, and I lurched after him. Peering back down the road, I could see no one, but I knew it wouldn't be long.

Ryan dug a pocketknife out of his jeans and plunged it into a truck tire. Escaping air hissed as he pulled it out.

"What are you doing?"

"Like you said, they'll know we ran out of gas. They'll bring some. Hopefully flat tires will slow them down. Here, slash the others." He handed me the knife.

I knelt down by the truck's wheel well and struggled to push the knife into the flat part of the tire near the hubcap. By grabbing a handy fist-sized rock and hammering on the knife's end, I was able to drive it far enough in to do the damage we needed. While I worked, Ryan jumped into the truck bed and pulled off the bungee cords holding the drum.

"Now what are you doing?"

"Maybe we can hide this somewhere and come back for it later."

"Ryan, look around." I gestured to the surrounding area. There was nothing but flat, barren ground dotted with sagebrush as far as we could see. "There's nowhere to hide it. We've got to get as far away from here as we can, and we can't drag this bomb with us. No way."

"We can't just leave it here for them. They'll get the truck running and head straight to Utah with it." Ryan's voice was anguished.

"Our only chance is to stay alive long enough to warn people," I said. "We'll have to leave it. At least they won't take the time to bother following us. I hope."

"Where should we go? Back to camp?"

"Let's go back for the motorcycle. Then we probably ought to head straight for Utah to warn them. We can't be that many miles from Snowville—it's right at the border. Hopefully they'll have a way to get in touch with the right people. I wish we could let the camp know I'm okay, but there isn't time."

I cringed when I thought of how frantic my family would be now that it was day and they'd seen I was gone. The leaders would be organizing searches, no doubt. What if they crossed paths with the bad guys?

CHAPTER SEVENTEEN

I LOOKED BEHIND US A million times as we left the freeway. I hustled to keep up with Ryan as we angled away from the road we'd driven on, back across the desert to the bike. So far, there was no sign of people in any direction. I didn't know if the terrorists would stick to the road, focusing on the truck, or cut through the desert to find us first.

When we pulled the bike out from its hiding place, Ryan jumped on and patted the seat behind him. "Let me try to drive it," he said. "It didn't look too hard."

"Now?"

"Yeah, now."

"Well, okay. At least there isn't much to crash into." I pointed out the clutch, the throttle, and the brakes.

"Yeah, yeah, let me try," he said impatiently. I climbed on behind him.

He didn't do too badly. We lurched a bit to begin with, but then we were rumbling over the desert in good time; however, I noticed he was going back toward camp rather than toward Utah.

"Where are you going?" I shouted over the roar of the engine.

"Our biggest problem is having enough gas to get all the way to Utah," Ryan shouted back. "I'm hoping there's still gas in that airplane."

"Maybe. Wouldn't be regular gas though."

"Might work in a pinch. Let's see if there's any in the tank."

In a few minutes, we pulled up beside the downed plane.

"We'll have to start a siphon," I said. "We'll need a hose of some kind and a container."

Ryan scrambled into the plane's cockpit and emerged a minute later with a two-liter pop bottle and another larger water container that might hold a couple of gallons.

We scavenged a hose from the plane's engine. "You do the siphon," I said. "Yuck."

Ryan grinned. "Okay, okay, Miss Dirtbike Farmgirl."

Ryan got a siphon started, and we both let out a whoop when golden liquid started flowing into the container. We managed to fill them both.

"I'm chicken to fill the motorcycle tank. What if this kind of gas won't work?" I said. "That would spoil the gas that's left in it."

"Either this gas works, or we're toast," Ryan said. "Fill 'er up." I poured gas from the pop bottle into the motorcycle, slopping only a little, and then we refilled the pop bottle.

I held my breath while Ryan kicked the starter, but the engine sputtered to life, sounding pretty much like it always had. "Thank goodness!"

I climbed back on behind him, wedging the containers of gas between us. I tried not to think about how dangerous that was.

Ryan aimed the bike toward camp.

"Now where are you going?"

"I'm taking you back. It's too dangerous, Amélie. I'm going to drop you off close to camp, and then I'm going on to Ogden alone."

"What?" I screeched.

"I'm sorry, Amèlie. Those guys are going to try to kill anyone who knows their plan. The only way is to get in front of them and warn the military. I've got to go fast, and I can do it faster on my own."

"You're taking up precious time. Turn around!"

"We're getting pretty close to my original hiding spot for the bike. It's not far from there to camp."

"Turn this bike around. Every second counts."

I yelled at him some more and even beat my fists uselessly on his back, but he paid me no heed until we got back to the big sagebrush where he'd first hidden the bike. He pulled up and shut off the bike. We both climbed off.

"Look, I feel terrible about this," he said. "I'm sending you to the wolves, making you face the leaders alone. But we have to split up. If we both get killed, no one will know about those guys. You've got to tell the camp. I've got to go on to Utah. If I go any closer to camp, they'll catch us. Then we'll have to explain, then they'll have to make a plan, and then they'll have to get volunteers and all that. It will take too long. I've just got to go now, go quick."

"And you don't need a cripple girl to slow you down."

"Amélie!" Ryan's voice was rough. "It's not like that." He put his hands on my arms. "I'm scared, Amélie. I'm scared for you too. I can't stand the thought of them shooting at you."

"Well, hurry, get out of here, then," I said, heavy with bitterness.

"Amélie . . . please . . . I'm no hero. Stay safe. Please." Ryan's hands traveled from my arms across my back, pulling me close, and then he pressed his lips against mine in a sweet, swift gesture. Heat prickled my cheeks.

"You still owe me," he whispered. Then he was gone.

* * *

I picked up my cane from under the sagebrush where I'd left it. Ryan must have been surprised I hadn't fought harder to go with him, but he was right. Although the thought made me burn with anger and shame, I'd only slow him down. It made sense that we split up in case something didn't go right with his plan.

His plan? What plan?

Still, I dreaded going back to the wolves without him. I couldn't imagine facing my mom after what I'd surely put her through. And President Green. I'd hoped to look grown-up and responsible in his eyes. That was pretty much ruined now.

Thoughts of what Zack would think were far too raw to acknowledge. I pushed them away. And for the first time on the entire journey, I was glad Dad wasn't around so he wouldn't have to be ashamed of me.

I trudged off toward camp, exhaustion from being awake all night overcoming the adrenaline that had pushed me on until now. Then a faint reminder of the day's significance flashed through my mind: Independence Day—how coincidental. I hoped that significance would last. I let the thought go, too tired to let the gravity of the situation process any further. It was getting close to midday, and I instead wondered if the group was on the move or if they'd stayed put to find me.

Either way, I figured it wouldn't be long until they spotted me. Sure enough, two men on horseback came over a rise and saw me immediately. One raised a bugle and gave three short blasts. They galloped over to me.

"Amélie! Are you all right?" one man asked. I recognized him from the Toppenish Ward.

"Yes, I'm fine. But I need to speak to President Green right away," I replied. I hoped the urgency of my message would forestall the embarrassing questions that surely bubbled in their minds.

He gave me a hand up onto the horse's back, and I settled in behind his saddle, holding my cane across my lap. He chirped to the horse, and we thundered across the desert to where the camp now marched.

President Green walked in a large group that included Mom and my brothers. I saw Zack on the fringe. I was glad they were together. Now I didn't have to decide whether it was more urgent to let my family know I was okay or tell President Green about the bomb.

As Mom threw her arms around my neck, crying and babbling about wicked kidnappers, it hit me that no one knew I'd snuck out of camp with Ryan Cook. And they wouldn't unless I told them. Everyone assumed I'd been kidnapped again. The temptation to make up a story like that was nearly impossible to resist.

I'd face that decision later, I told myself. Right now, I had a message that needed telling.

"President Green, I'm sorry for the worry I've caused." I gently extracted myself from Mom's tangling arms. "I have important news and"—I looked meaningfully at the people who'd gathered at my appearance—"it would probably be best if we talked alone."

President Green nodded. He put an arm around my shoulders and drew me to the side of the road. "I'm overjoyed to see you're okay," he said. "Now what's this all about?"

I drew a deep breath. "This is going to sound wacky. But . . . there are some men, two at least, who are trying to take a bomb to Ogden, Utah. I'm pretty sure they intend to set it off at the air force base there."

President Green's face blanched. "What? How do you know that?"

"You remember Ryan Cook?"

"Yes. The singer, the one who's made himself so scarce lately."

I shamefacedly told him how I'd snuck out of camp with Ryan and found the airplane and the abandoned house—and stolen the truck with the bomb intended for Ogden. "Now Ryan's on a motorcycle racing for Utah right now. He's trying to get there before these men. But I'm really scared for him, President. They'll do anything to stop him. They'll kill him if they can."

I could see the wheels turning in the president's mind while he asked me about a few more details. "All right. I have to talk to the captains. Please don't go anywhere. I'll need you."

"Okay. But President—we have to hurry. Ryan—"

"We'll work as fast as we can, sister." President Green squeezed my arm and then strode back to the people he'd been walking with. "Stop the group immediately," I heard him call. "Gather the captains."

There hadn't been a reason to stop the caravan in the middle of the day before, so I was impressed to see how swiftly it happened. A bugler gave two short blasts, paused, and repeated the pattern several times. Almost immediately the huge, sprawling group ground to a stop. I smiled when I realized the two short blasts resembled the "pause" button on my iPod.

Men on horseback galloped up, spilling out of their saddles and tossing reins to people standing by. These were the captains of one hundred, and they gathered around President Green and me.

The captains eyed me curiously, but President Green held up a hand. "Sister Hatch has brought urgent news." He gestured for me to speak.

I swallowed nervously. These people would think Mom's crazy genes had finally taken over. "Some men have a bomb. They're trying to take it to Ogden to set it off."

"Are you kidding?" a captain asked. "Is it related to the EMP bomb?"

"I don't know. It's not up in the atmosphere, though, like that one."

"Why bother? The country's already upside down."

President Green coughed. "The emergency ham radio network confirmed that the government is trying to reform there."

"What? Are you kidding?" a captain said. "In Utah? Why there?"

"Frankly, there's not much choice. Most metropolitan areas in the country are pretty wiped out. But that's a discussion for another time.

"A young man from our camp—Ryan Cook—is already headed for Utah to warn them. He needs backup. And we need a separate group to intercept these bombers. The main body isn't going another step closer to Utah until that bomb is taken care of."

"Ryan Cook? We're acting on his word?"

"It's true!" I blurted out. "We saw their plane and everything. We heard them. We saw the bomb. They shot at us!"

"We're doing this," President Green said firmly.

"How many men do we need?" another captain asked.

"Not many. Speed is the most important thing. We'll need at least three pickups with six men each. One to back up Brother Cook and the others to go straight to Ogden."

"I'll need to go with them," I said as firmly as I could manage.

No one seemed to hear me.

"Brethren, who do you have in your companies with military experience? Each captain pick your best man and report back in fifteen minutes. Let's get this show on the road. Brother Roundy, you're in charge of making assignments."

Mom handed me a couple of pieces of bread while the group formed. I squeezed her arm gratefully and ate, but the bread sat like a lump of wet clay in my stomach. How could a person be so scared and yet so eager to do something at the same time?

When the men had gathered, I described the bomb and the two terrorists the best I could. Brother Roundy chose some men to go after Ryan. They filled the truck's tank with precious gas and sped out of camp. My heart leapt after them. *Hurry, brethren, hurry!*

Brother Roundy started assigning the remaining men into groups. I realized with growing panic that I wasn't being included.

"Wait! Which group will I be with?"

Looking down at me with a kind smile, Brother Roundy said, "That's okay, dear. We've got it."

"No, I have to go. I have to! Ryan's my friend."

"I'm sorry, Amélie," he said. He had the nerve to glance at my leg. "There's just no way that's going to work. We'll take care of it, I promise."

In the movie version, I'd be the girl MacGyver, cutting the red wire when the timer had 00:01 left on the readout. But in real life, I was to be left behind. Not to be scorned but pitied. That was reality.

My hand squeezed around my cane until my fingers cramped. It's ironic that even though the bottom half of my left leg was a small percentage of my body, it was running the whole show. My cane was like an exclamation point declaring, "Watch out! Damaged!" Without it, I could almost pretend I was whole.

No! I screamed inside my head. I clenched the cane even tighter. I imagined it snapping with the force of my grip. *I deny you. You. Are. Not. Who. I. Am.*

If my life were a movie, this would have been the big moment of clarity. The music would swell. "All I have to do is believe!" I'd crow triumphantly. I'd hurl the cane away. Off it would spin, end over end. Then I'd break into a run, my legs unchained at last.

But this was no movie. This was the real-life version.

Tears streamed down my face as I watched the groups depart. For the thousandth time, I thought of Dad. My mind recycled all of the hurt feelings about him being gone when I'd really needed him. For the thousandth time, I thought that if Dad were here, it wouldn't be like this.

I felt like a dry husk, a corncob left on the stalk through the winter, shriveled and puny. I couldn't remember if I'd ever had a father or if that was just a pleasant dream—a dream where I didn't walk every day, all day, a dream where I opened a refrigerator and saw it bursting with cold, delicious food, a dream where my father was there with his strong arms around me, carrying me.

My eyes blurred, and I saw Dad's face as he knelt beside me, his knees digging into the gravel of our driveway, tears pouring down his weathered face while he pulled me out from underneath the Bluebird. I felt the seeping trickle of holy oil and his hands lying heavy and warm on my head. I felt him scoop me up and carry me, my face pressed against the soft flannel of his shirt.

How many times had he carried me?

I closed my eyes. I felt my spirit struggle to reach out. A dribble of warmth entered my heart and then poured over me in a gush.

There was a Father with me.

I knew. My job in the Ryan Recovery Mission was to have faith. In a still, small voice, Father whispered to me that my part wasn't a stupid left-over job, only good enough for cripples. It was the most important job I could have.

Maybe I couldn't run, but I could pray.

I turned, scrubbed my wet cheeks with the backs of my hands, and hugged Mom hard.

Then I got busy.

* * *

Ryan and the men came back the next day. I hadn't seen them yet, but the story flew across camp that they'd successfully ambushed the terrorists before they got to the air force base. Everyone was safe. It turned out that the bomb wasn't a nuke after all but only a "dirty bomb"—much less destructive but still something that would have rendered the base unusable for a new seat of government. Our men found the bad guys near Ogden, so I guessed they'd scavenged new tires from another vehicle. Our men had disarmed the bomb before it'd had a chance to blow its payload of radioactive debris across the base.

Night fell, and the happy crowd around Ryan dissipated. No fireworks, but it still felt like a party. It all seemed a little too fitting for Independence Day; I personally preferred the fireworks to the actual fight for freedom, but I was thankful Ryan and the others had done so much to keep us safe. I walked over to the fire pit where he'd held court. The face I'd seen plastered on lockers and notebooks three months ago had changed. Dark curls still dangled roguishly across his brows, and his features were still pop-star perfect. But his eyes had looked upon things that had forever changed them.

"Ryan, you're okay. You did it!" I grinned at him. He reached out and drew me close.

I started to ask him a hundred questions. I tried to tell him I'd prayed for him. Instead of letting me speak, he kissed me, his lips sweet and skillful. He took his time, his hands stroking my hair, my face. He played me like a rare, fragile guitar.

I couldn't breathe.

"There," he whispered. "Now you're paid up."

He slipped away into the desert night without another word.

CHAPTER EIGHTEEN

Thursday, July 5

THE NEXT MORNING I STUMBLED down I-84 in a haze. We'd been walking for thirty-eight days. It seemed more like two thousand years.

There was nothing to look at but stretches of dry, colorless land. No towns, no farms. No churches.

Ryan passed me, turning to wink and wave. I blushed. I had no idea how to act. After all, he wasn't the same Ryan anymore. He couldn't be. He'd looked death in the eye and come back to us. And what about that kiss? It had felt like the kind of kiss a guy gave a girl he really cared about.

Mom walked beside me, her skirt swishing around her ankles.

"Have you talked to Zack lately?"

"Of course not." I snorted.

"How long has it been?"

"Two weeks."

"You know, you ought to talk to him—start over with him. You guys have been friends too long. And haven't you noticed? He looks perfectly miserable all the time. He needs a friend."

"Mom!" I exclaimed. "He dumped me! Without even bothering to explain! He should be miserable. He deserves it."

Mom made little clucking noises with her tongue and turned her head to look at someone. I knew she was looking at Zack.

I tried. Oh, heaven, how I tried to stop myself. But my eyes helplessly followed.

Good, I thought. *Zack does look miserable*. He walked alone, as usual these days, hands stuffed in pockets, head down. His face had the look of someone doing all he could to grit his teeth and hang on, to simply endure.

What had happened? Why couldn't he explain? He wouldn't want to say he'd found me loathsome—too kind to go that far. But his supposed kindness hadn't prevented him from breaking my heart.

"I thought you were different, Zack," I muttered under my breath. "But you're not. You're just like all the rest."

And what about the Church thing? I'd been sure all he'd have to do was read the Book of Mormon. Then the magic would take over. Wasn't that what was promised in Moroni? Why hadn't it worked? Why had he been given a lifesaving miracle a hundred times more rare and amazing than anything I'd ever seen before but not the simple confirmation about the Church—the thing everyone was supposed to be able to get? The thing that by its very nature was supposed to be not rare at all?

A commotion ahead pulled me out of my frustrated thoughts. A clog of people had gathered on the side of the freeway a few hundred yards down, and they were all clamoring over something. Others ran toward them.

"What now?" I asked. Mom shrugged. My steps grew heavier as I anticipated yet another problem I felt too worn out to face. But when we got closer, I saw that it wasn't a new calamity.

The cluster of people capered around a "Welcome to Utah" sign. The cacophony I'd heard was laughing and shouting, nothing more. I smiled despite my irritable mood. I found myself wishing we had a camera to document the moment. But now that cameras were digital, none of them worked. Who had an old film camera anymore? No one I knew.

We'd made it! At least to the Utah border. I knew from my previous car trips that Salt Lake City was only a hundred miles or so farther. A handful of days.

I wondered yet again what it would be like when we got to Church headquarters. I assumed they'd have some sort of temporary shelter for us, and in some respects, that would be similar to camping in a church somewhere. But the walking. At least that would be over.

That night we stopped at a church in Snowville, and after a meager supper, a dance spontaneously started on the overgrown lawn. The same musicians I'd lined up before played, Ryan included. I went nowhere near that scene. I didn't want to be reminded of how happy I'd been with Zack the night of the first dance. And no way did I want to see Ryan playing his guitar. The last thing I needed was another brain-scrambling by the Ryan Cook Magic Show.

About a half hour or so into the dance, President Green and the missionaries stepped up in front of the band, and President Green raised his megaphone.

"Glad to see everyone having a good time." His gaze flicked past the shadows where I sat. "It's great to pass this milestone and be on Utah soil. And I have some news I think you'll be excited about. Zack Allman, would you step over here with me, please?"

The crowd hushed. I stared. What on earth? Zack threaded his way to the president's side.

"Tomorrow night we should reach the Bear River, where something very special will happen. This young man will be baptized."

The crowd erupted with cheers while President Green shook Zack's hand and then enveloped him in a hug. The missionaries pounded his back with friendly thumps.

My jaw dropped. I couldn't speak. Baptized? Zack? How did this happen? And why was I the last to know?

The musicians began playing again, and I waited for Zack to finally seek me out to give an explanation. But he never approached me in my dark corner; the dance ended, and people drifted to their bedrolls. Disappointment lanced through me.

Get over it, I scolded myself, pulling my blankets over my head. *This is real life. Get used to it.*

The next day was filled with more dreary walking. I spent the time alternately praying for and cursing Zack.

Of course I was happy for him. It was wonderful. The magic had happened. But, oh, how it hurt that I hadn't been a part of it, that I'd been cruelly shoved to the side while Zack made this discovery without me. How I would have loved to be there with him when his faith was born, while it grew to the point that he could make this commitment.

Why, oh, why, hadn't he wanted me there?

The next time I saw Zack, he was sitting on the bank of the Bear River, dressed in a white shirt and someone's temple pants. An unknown helper had cut his hair short, the way he liked it. A little line of pale skin showed around the edges of his hairline.

Masses of people spread out on the riverbank, maybe even the whole camp. Who'd want to miss this? I found a place with Mom and the boys somewhere in the middle.

Zack turned his head to speak to Elder Robertson next to him, and I caught a glimpse of his face in profile. He looked calm yet determined.

What was going through that head of his? Was he happy about being baptized? Could he feel the Spirit confirming his choice?

Normally, I adored attending baptisms, even of little eight-year-olds. I felt the Spirit there like nowhere else. The words of the baptismal prayer always rang in my ears like chapel bells, full of promise and portent. I hoped I'd feel the same way today, in spite of feeling abandoned by Zack.

I looked at Mom and the boys next to me. At least I still had them. That would never change.

We sang "There Is a Green Hill Far Away," and Elder Shaw gave a short talk on the baptismal covenant. So far, things were exactly like every baptism I'd ever attended—except for the fact that we all sat on the ground facing a river instead of the baptismal font in the stake center.

Then Elder Robertson stood, also dressed from head to toe in white. Earlier in the day, the leaders had fired up the ham radio and found a Church member living nearby who had some baptismal clothing from his own baptism. One of the stake men had ridden out on horseback and borrowed the clothes. The elder now held a hand out to Zack, pulling him to his feet. They walked side by side down into the river, the current swirling around them.

Elder Robertson paused when they were up to their waist in water and gently turned Zack to face us. Then the missionary raised his right arm to the square and recited the baptismal prayer.

My heart thundered.

Elder Robertson buried Zack in the water and raised him again, water streaming off Zack's brow and shoulders. He glanced quickly at the witnesses, who nodded. Zack had been completely immersed.

The Spirit filled me so full it almost hurt. I cried helplessly, and all around me snifflings and sobs let me know others felt it too.

Elder Robertson and Zack sloshed onto the bank. My eyes fastened on Zack's, and to my surprise, he looked steadily back at me, the water on his face renewed by tears.

I thought of my own baptism as a young child. Despite my age, I'd felt the Spirit's piercings then too. *Feel it, Zack,* I silently pleaded. *Drink it in. This is the moment in your life when you are allowed to feel like a pure, holy angel. Never forget.*

Someone produced a camp chair and set it up on the uneven ground. Others handed towels to the dripping young men. Elder Robertson led

Zack to the chair. President Green, Bishop Taylor, the missionaries, and a few others formed a circle and laid their hands on Zack's head. I could barely see him now, but I caught a glimpse of his face as he looked up in wonder at the faces surrounding him.

What's this like for him? I remembered how it felt when I'd been confirmed—the hands warm and heavy on my head, the solid wall of priesthood circling me like a bulwark. I'd seen it many times before it was my turn. But for Zack, this was the first.

The prayer ended, and one by one, the men in the circle embraced Zack. The people in the congregation rose—some going forward to greet Zack, some drifting off toward camp. I lingered in my spot on the riverbank.

Zack caught my eye a couple of times as he went through the Mormon Handshake and Hug Express. His expression seemed to say, "Wait for me, Lee-Lee. Don't move."

I rubbed my temples. My poor mind couldn't figure Zack out. Apparently he had something to say to me at long last. I was tempted to rebuff him, to hurt him back. I smarted from his lousy treatment of me, and although I was elated for his baptism, I was angry. Very angry. I nearly walked away with the others to force him to come find me, chase me down. But my curiosity about what he'd say tied me to the spot. That and the fact that the riverbank was pretty uneven and I'd probably trip and fall in my attempt to stalk away in a haughty huff. That'd spoil the effect.

"Want some help up?" Mom stood and put out a hand.

"Huh?" I'd totally forgotten she'd been sitting beside me. "Uh, no, I'm going to hang out here for a while."

"Okay." Mom smiled and squeezed my shoulder as she left.

The last happy hugger thumped Zack's back and wandered away. Zack immediately turned and made a beeline for where I sat. I suppressed a little squeak of nervousness.

"Hey," he said, sitting beside me.

"Hey," I replied, trying to keep my voice noncommittal. Not furious but not implying forgiveness either. "Are you cold?" It was a warm June morning, but he was soaking wet.

"Naw." He fidgeted with some cheatgrass growing along the riverbank. "I did it, Lee-Lee. I made it. I got baptized."

Funny choice of words, I thought. "I'm really happy for you, Zack."

Zack shifted so he was sitting cross-legged, facing me. "Lee, I know I've hurt you. I don't know if you can ever forgive me. But please give me a chance to explain. I'm finally at a point where I can try. It won't excuse me, and it may not make sense, but I'd like to try."

"Okay." My answer was clipped.

"First off, you've gotta know how weird this whole thing with the Church felt at first. You know how Dad was about it. I know it sounds silly, but it felt disloyal." He paused and peered at me, his eyes hopeful.

I shrugged. "Doesn't seem silly to me that you'd feel like that."

I knew if I looked at him, he'd be wrinkling the skin between his brows the way he always did when he was figuring out how to say something. I knew his face better than my own. All of his expressions, happy, sad, angry, bored—I'd seen them all a million times. *I know you inside and out, Zack Allman*, I thought. *But I don't know what you're going to say, not this time.* I kept my eyes on the ground.

"But then the disaster happened—and things changed between us— and I decided I'd better find out, once and for all, about this Mormon stuff. I wanted it to work between us, Lee. More than anything."

I stared at the most interesting little spot of dirt between my holey shoes.

"At first, the lessons with the missionaries were just sort of a diversion. Something to do. I never thought anything would really come of it. I'd stay loyal. It wasn't hard to think that way at first. I mean, come on, the whole gold plates thing and visions and angels and everything. I thought Joseph Smith was crazy and I'd be a wack-job to believe that stuff.

"But everything was wrapped up together with you, Lee. You believed it. I knew you took it seriously. And like I told you before, I knew if I wanted to get serious with you, I'd have to take your religion seriously too. I wondered if there was a way I could be a Mormon for you but keep my inner heart loyal to my dad and to the Catholic Church."

I stole a tiny glance Zack's way. He looked resigned, his fingers still picking away at the bunch of grass he'd pulled.

"I kept reading the Book of Mormon, but every time I did, it felt like blasphemy. I wondered if I was putting my eternal soul in jeopardy just to be with you."

That thought rocked me back on my proverbial heels. I stared at him openly this time.

"I thought maybe it wouldn't be so bad, playing Mormon, if it meant I could keep you. I thought maybe if I didn't think about it too much, it'd be okay. Then I remembered what you said about how for you, it had to be real. No faking it."

Zack scrubbed his hand through his damp hair. "For the first time, I tried to honestly pray about this stuff, and guess what, Lee? I felt something. Something different than I'd felt ever before. My first thought was, 'Oh, no! What if this really is true?' It scared me. Then I thought, 'Yes! It is true, and I can stay with Lee.' I was a mixed-up kid. Somehow, I had to know for sure. I had to know for real.

"I tried my hardest to separate you from the Church in my mind. But I just couldn't do it. I couldn't feel whether it was true or if I just wanted it to be true. For you. So I had to separate myself from you. It was the only way for me to know for sure whether it was my own mind talking or not. I knew you'd be hurt. I knew you'd be angry. But that's why I did it, Lee, and I didn't dare explain anything to you until I made it under the water. So it'd be real.

"Now, I don't blame you if you can't forgive me. I hope and pray you will, but either way, I'm a Mormon, inside and out. For real, forever."

Tears ran down both of our faces. Zack reached out a hand to me, tentative, hopeful. I tried to think of a reason to stay mad at him. I couldn't. I couldn't think at all.

I flew into his arms, and then things were really, really all better again.

CHAPTER NINETEEN

Friday, July 6

ZACK CRIED FOR A LONG time—to the point that it started to get awkward. It did feel nice that he was so relieved about me forgiving him that he'd cry. Much nicer than feeling rejected.

Turns out, I was only one reason why he couldn't stop crying. It was beginning to sink in that his baptism washed away all of his sins, including shooting the guy in his dad's pickup. Apparently, during his baptismal interview, he'd been pretty sure that was going to be a deal breaker and the Church wouldn't take him.

"But it was Jesus who took me," he said, his voice soft and awed.

"You're feeling it. You're really feeling it." I couldn't stop grinning.

"Oh yeah. It's real."

* * *

The next day, somewhere north of Ogden, an old car drove up the highway toward us. A buzz—no, it was more like a roar—swept through the group when word spread that the car carried messengers from Salt Lake City. Two men in suits spoke with President Green for a few minutes, and then the car returned the way it had come.

Out came the megaphone. "Brothers and sisters, the time has come for our stake to go separate ways," President Green said, his face solemn. "Host families have been set up to take groups in as we pass through the several towns on our way south. The captains will let you know when it's your turn to leave the group."

He passed a weathered hand over his face. "God only knows when we'll be together again as a stake. Perhaps never. But I'll always cherish the memory of serving as your leader, and I want you to know I love each of you. May God's blessings be with you all."

There was a moment of stunned silence, and then a cheer spread across the stake like a wave—a cheer for President Green. He'd brought us through—like a shepherd and his unruly sheep. Like Brigham Young. I chuckled to myself.

When we got to Ogden, fifty or so people left the group, nearly all green-truck riders. Some of them looked pretty haggard from the journey and happy to finally be at the end. As we went south, more of the older and sicker people's names were called until there was hardly anyone left on the green truck.

Bishop Taylor caught up with me. "You know, Amélie, you could ride that truck now without anyone thinking a thing. You always could have but especially now."

I laughed. "Are you kidding? I've come this far. I'm not going to buckle now. Besides, I'll bet my name is called before too many more miles, since they seem to be choosing the sick and the slow."

"Actually, you're scheduled to stay with the group to the very end—clear into Salt Lake City."

That surprised me. A hundred questions crowded my head. How long had he known that? Why was I to continue on? I was one of the slowest. Was it the luck of the draw or a particular reason? I knew my family would stick together, but what about Zack?

"Why us?" I blurted.

"I couldn't say," Bishop Taylor said, patting my shoulder as he turned away. *Couldn't or wouldn't*, I wondered.

Another couple hundred people peeled off from the group before we stopped for the night at a church in Centerville. The sheer number of churches to pick from blew my mind after having to walk such a long way between them for the last couple of months. Practically one on every corner.

The next day, Sunday, supper was a crazy hodgepodge of the food we had left. It was our very last supper together. Tomorrow we'd be in Salt Lake City.

After we ate we filed into the chapel alight with the flicker of candles. As I sat down between Mom and Zack, I thought I'd never seen a prettier chapel. It looked magical.

I leaned over and whispered in Mom's ear, "Remember that rule about no open flames in the church?" We grinned at each other. That was one rule that had been broken over and over again in the past few months.

The meeting followed standard Mormon procedure. A song, a prayer. I played the piano as usual. I felt a little twinge of sadness that I'd no longer be President Green's go-to girl.

President Green opened the meeting to testimonies. Several people hurried to the stand, and I felt Zack squirm beside me.

"Am I expected to do that?" he whispered as one person after another tearfully bore their testimony.

"You can, but you don't have to. There will be lots more chances—a whole lifetime of them," I said.

Zack breathed out a deep sigh and settled back against the bench.

Mom nudged me and pointed with her eyes at the aisle. Ryan walked past our row to the front.

All Ryan's brash stage presence seemed to have fled. He bowed his head before the mute microphone for a moment then looked out across the congregation, raking a hand through his hair.

"I just want to tell everyone thanks," he said. "Thank you for letting me come along even though I haven't been the best churchgoer in the past. I didn't think I needed that in my life, but being in this group has changed my mind. You people are some of the finest I've ever met. You make me want to be a better person. It's hard to think of being separated from all of you. I'll always think of you as my family." He turned and reached a hand out to President Green. They shook hands warmly, and then Ryan hurried from the stand.

As the meeting ended, I realized I'd rarely felt such an intense mixture of happy and sad. Maybe never.

* * *

In the morning, old trucks and cars began arriving, loading up hundreds of people bound for wards in various suburbs of Salt Lake City. I looked with curiosity at the remaining group. What was the common denominator? I saw the stake leaders and the captains of one hundred. I supposed that was logical. But the rest? There were ten or fifteen families, a mix of young and old, plus a few random people like Zack and Ryan, perhaps forty altogether.

"Well, here we are, the stragglers," President Green said. "We'll be going on downtown. Everyone climb on—we're going in style." He motioned to the green truck.

Everyone else moved toward the truck, but my legs froze in place.

The green truck.

It doesn't mean what it once did, I told myself. *It's only an old, beat-up truck. It's not a symbol or an omen or anything but a rusted-out tin box on wheels.*

Zack linked his arm through mine. "C'mon, Lee-Lee," he said. "It's okay."

It was as if his touch broke me out of the trance. "Well, I guess if you are all going to wimp out, I'll have to follow," I said with a grin.

Before I could think, Zack moved behind me, put his hands on my waist, and lifted me up onto the flatbed. I squeaked in surprise.

"Whoa, Zack! Hope you didn't hurt your back or something!"

"Pshaw. Same as a bale of hay."

Zack and I settled ourselves between Mom and the boys. Ryan waggled his fingers at me from across the truck bed. Girls sat on each side of him.

We drove down the nearly empty freeway, getting off at an exit marked 600 North. It seemed strange to speed down the road and to see an occasional vehicle pass us. I gazed up at the tall office buildings towering over the street. Did people still work inside, even though there was no electricity? Did they huff and puff up nine flights of stairs to sit behind dark computer monitors?

The streets thronged with pedestrians, and I smiled to see a few horse-drawn carts. I remembered why the Salt Lake blocks were laid out with such pleasantly wide streets—Brigham Young wanted them wide enough to U-turn a full team of horses. It seemed the city had come full circle.

The green truck pulled up in front of the Lion House, a downtown landmark I remembered from previous trips to Utah. I'd eaten in the restaurant on the bottom floor a few times.

"Welcome, brothers and sisters." A middle-aged woman, whose severe blue suit, strained at its buttons, greeted us, sweeping her arm toward the Lion House's entry. "Please come inside."

We filed toward the door. I was suddenly aware of my grimy T-shirt and jeans with mud-encrusted hems. A few others paused to whack at their clothes before crossing the threshold.

We'd made it. We were dirty, we were tired, we were bedraggled, but we were actually here. Salt Lake City.

Our matronly guide ushered us up a flight of stairs. The forty of us shuffled into a banquet room set with long tables, and wonderful smells floated over to us from a sideboard piled with food. Real food—white-flour pastries, cuts of meat roasted and sliced onto a plate instead of stewed in a big pot, colorful vegetables dripping with butter. We drifted toward it like a forty-headed amoeba.

"Help yourselves, folks," the woman said. "Elder Stoddard will be in shortly to speak with you."

After a hasty prayer, we fell on the food. A man I assumed was Elder Stoddard came in. He was apparently a General Authority of some sort and walked around the room greeting each of us.

"Thanks so much for the part each of you played in bringing your stake safely to Utah. Enjoy the food, and I'll be back in a moment to give you some instructions on where you'll be housed. In the meantime, may I have the Hatch family follow me for a moment?" He gestured toward the door.

I looked at Mom and the boys, stunned. What was going on? Mom shrugged. I shot a glance at Zack, but he waved me on. We trooped after Elder Stoddard.

Once in the hallway, the man said, "Sorry to interrupt your dinner, but there's someone I think you'd like to see without any more delay."

He stopped before a closed door, turned the knob, and opened it.

Inside sat Dad.

CHAPTER TWENTY

Monday, July 9

MOM LET OUT A STRANGLED little scream and hurled herself at Dad; the boys and I were right behind. We clutched each other for a few sweet moments, and Mom wasn't the only one crying.

We finally released each other. I realized Elder Stoddard wasn't in the room with us but had discreetly withdrawn.

Dad spoke first. "Thank God you're all safe. It's been a long three months worrying about you guys."

Mom nodded, her sobs subsiding into huge gulps.

For a little while, all we could do was look at each other, touch each other. Dad was really there! It wasn't a dream or me wishing so hard for something that I'd conjured up an illusion. He was real. He looked exactly the same, which struck me as odd. But we had only been apart a few months, not years.

Then all at once, the questions started.

"Tina, my love, how long have you been in Salt Lake? Have you boys grown a whole foot each since I last saw you? Lee-Lee, what's this they tell me about you being kidnapped?"

"Dad, where have you been? Why was it a secret? Can you tell us now? What's going on?"

Dad motioned behind him, and for the first time, I noticed the room was furnished with squishy chairs and couches. "Yes, I have permission to talk about what I've been doing the last few months. I'm eager to fill you in."

We sat down, pulling chairs up so we were in a tight circle, knees touching. It was as if no one wanted to let go of each other or someone might disappear.

Dad drew a deep breath and paused. I thought I'd burst from curiosity.

"Spit it out, Dad," Ethan said, edging even closer.

"I've been working on a special building project for the Church."

"Building project? But you're a farmer," I said.

"Among other things, I worked on a new grain storage facility."

"Uh . . . okay. I guess that makes sense, sort of."

"They called in farmers and ag people from all over the country," Dad said. "Besides the big silos, we supervised spring planting of several thousand acres of Church land."

"Whoa! Sounds big," I said. "But, Dad, I still don't understand why that would be such a secret. Sounds like something I'd expect the Church to do, not some big hush-hush thing."

"It's not the *what* that was a secret. It's the *where*," Dad said. "The storage facility is part of a huge complex of buildings going up in . . . Jackson County."

Realization dawned on me. I swallowed. Jackson County! In seminary, I'd learned that an important phase in the Second Coming of the Lord Jesus Christ would happen there. "The temple," I whispered. "They're building *the* temple, aren't they?"

"Yes. We're in the middle of a prophecy coming to pass."

Shivers ran up and down my arms. Ethan and Jarron gaped, their mouths hanging open. Mom looked at her feet. She'd known.

"Why couldn't you tell us?" I looked from Mom to Dad.

"Plans were made years ago for this project," Dad replied. "Way before the attacks. The leaders decided this should go forward in secrecy so obstacles from the government and so on could be overcome. The Church has been quietly buying land in the area for years. Also, they didn't want the members to go crazy while things were prepared. You know how people get. It would have been chaos if everyone knew about the temple."

"So you've been in Missouri?"

"Yep. The leaders let me come back to meet you. And we're not going to be separated ever again if I can help it."

"So what happens now?" I asked.

Dad turned to me. "Elder Stoddard would like to talk to us about that, and he said they have something specific in mind for you."

I gulped. "Elder Stoddard? Me? Why?" My stomach flip-flopped.

Dad stood and reached out a hand, drawing me to my feet. We all walked back to the banquet room and into the curious stares of our traveling companions. Most people in the stake knew by now that we had been fatherless. Zack's face lit up in recognition as he looked from me to Dad. He jumped to his feet.

Elder Stoddard crossed the room to us. "Glad to see the family back together," he said, smiling. He turned to me, and my skin crawled with nervousness. What could he possibly have to say to me? Was I in trouble for something?

"Sister Hatch, we owe you a special debt of gratitude for the part you played in bringing the Yakima Stake safely to Utah. We're very impressed by your bravery and spirit."

"Me?" I stammered.

"Yes. We'll need all the brave young people we can get in the next few years. As a matter of fact, we have a special assignment for you. As you know, the United States government is being reestablished here in Utah. This, among other reasons, has led to a big decision for the Church. We're relocating to Missouri. We'll leave Utah to the government and anyone else who wants to stay. It's not time for the entire Church to gather, but many thousands will be involved in this move. We'll need experienced people to help it go as smoothly as possible. The young people of the Church will have a special role to play in this move, and we'd like you to help organize it."

I was too stunned to speak and stood gaping like a trout on a riverbank.

Elder Stoddard laid a reassuring hand on my shoulder. I looked up at his kind, wrinkled face and tried to understand why he'd asked me—of all people—to do this.

My brain started to automatically spew its customary poison. *They've got me mixed up with someone else*, it said. *They can't mean me, the cripple girl. I can't do anything right! All I do is slow people down, weigh on them, burden them.*

But then something new, something grown-up rose inside me. I had done amazing things. Brave things. I'd done some good on our trek from Washington. I knew I could help with this new endeavor. I could serve the kingdom.

"I have only three questions. Will I have to leave my family?" I asked, forcing the quiver from my voice.

"No. We won't ask that of you. They'll be helping you."

"Oh. Okay. Good."

"What's your second question?"

"What does this assignment entail?"

Elder Stoddard's eyes twinkled. "We'll inform you of that very soon. Don't worry. You'll definitely be guided as you fulfill your role in strengthening and gathering the youth of the Church. And the third?"

"What about Zack Allman?"

He smiled. He seemed to know exactly whom I was talking about. "Zack will have his own mission to fulfill, but I dare say you'll run into each other from time to time."

* * *

Two days later, Zack and I sat by the reflecting pool on Temple Square. Deepening twilight slanted across the gardens that were still meticulously maintained.

I guess they don't need electricity to grow flowers, I thought. I looked at the reflection of the temple in the still, glasslike surface of the pool. Candlelight glowed in the temple windows, glimmering and rippling like fairy lights on the water.

"So tell me about your meeting," I said, picking up Zack's hand and lacing my fingers through his.

"They say a war is coming. They've asked the young men to form a militia. We're all joining. Even Ryan."

"A militia? The Church's own?"

"Yeah. They're going to call it the Nauvoo Legion. Weird name."

I laughed. "Too bad getting baptized doesn't provide you with an Automatic Mormontalk Translator."

My laugh fizzled as I pictured Zack in a military uniform, marching away to more danger. A shiver of fear ran through me.

Zack's eyes held mine. "I can't promise I'll be able to stay where you are, Lee-Lee. But that's where I want to be. That's where I'll try to be."

I shivered again but not from fear. "Is this it, Zack?"

"Sorry?"

"This feeling. Us. Is this the real thing? The forever thing?"

"You mean love, forever and ever, now, tomorrow, next month, all the time, on earth and in heaven?"

I nodded.

"This is as close to heaven as I ever expect to be."

Then Zack put his arms around me, and he held me for a million years.

About the Author

Margot Hovley was raised in rural Washington State, where she worked as a pig herder and champion produce-box maker. She now lives and plays in Utah with her big family. When she's not storytelling, she's hanging out with family, teaching music to the somewhat willing, and fooling around with techy gadgets. She loves hiking, traveling, and concocting adventures.

Margot loves to hear from readers. To send her praises, complaints, ideas, questions, or whining, please visit www.margothovley.com. She also welcomes readers to her popular self-reliance blog at www.mynewoldschool.com.